'What are you

Luc's eyes found he... brilliantly. 'Reconsidering my strategy,' he said. His voice was full of that infuriating secret amusement again.

To Christina's complete astonishment, he leaned down and slid the sunglasses down her nose so that he could speak straight into her suspicious eyes.

'Don't look so alarmed, Christina Howard.'

He bent his head before she knew what he was about and gave her a light, searing kiss full on her startled mouth.

Then he was gone, slipping like a shadow among the shadows of the waterfront buildings. Christina stared after him. The kiss had been so brief that she was not sure whether she had conjured it up from her fevered imagination. But then she touched her throbbing lips. It was not her imagination. God knew who he was or what he wanted but, whatever it was, he was *there*.

Irrationally, recklessly, her heart began to sing.

Born in London, **Sophie Weston** is a traveller by nature who started writing when she was five. She wrote her first romance when she was recovering from illness, thinking her travelling was over. She was wrong, but she enjoyed it so much that she carried on. These days she lives in the heart of the city with two demanding cats and a cherry tree—and travels the world looking for settings for her stories.

AVOIDING MR RIGHT

BY
SOPHIE WESTON

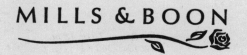

MILLS & BOON

*All the characters in this book have no existence outside the imagination
of the author, and have no relation whatsoever to anyone bearing the
same name or names. They are not even distantly inspired by any
individual known or unknown to the author, and all the incidents are
pure invention.*

*MILLS & BOON and the Rose Device
are trademarks of the publisher.
Harlequin Mills & Boon Limited,
Eton House, 18-24 Paradise Road, Richmond, Surrey TW9 1SR*

© Sophie Weston 1996

ISBN 0 263 79743 0

*Set in Times Roman 10 on 12 pt.
02-9610-57360 C1*

Made and printed in Great Britain

CHAPTER ONE

'I DON'T *believe* it.'

Christina glared impotently at the man on the other side of the bank's glass barrier. Behind her, she was conscious that the queue was getting impatient. Her opponent looked bored. He even shrugged.

'It's crazy,' she protested.

He was adamant. 'You should have made an arrangement. It is the rules.' He permitted himself a complacent smirk. 'The rules are for your own protection, Miss—er—Howard.'

There was no need for him to squint down àt her cash withdrawal form like that. He and Christina had been arguing about it for fifteen minutes. He must know her name as well as she knew it herself by now.

But he was a petty official with a point to make and he was enjoying himself. He was having fun pointing out that she was thoughtless and inefficient. Still, what else could you expect from a girl? his manner said. More important, his manner also said that he was the one in control here. And that he wasn't going to bend the rules even a little. Christina had strong views about men who liked to be in control and this man was reinforcing all of them.

'You certainly don't get your kicks out of helping your customers, do you?' Christina said sweetly.

She was beaten and she knew it. But she was not going to slink away without telling him exactly what she thought of him. Her self-respect demanded it.

He looked wary. This was where, in a perfect world, the bank manager would come out of his office and say,

5

'Christina, my dear girl, why didn't you tell me?' and sweep her off triumphant, leaving the petty clerk quaking. She sighed, shaking out her soft brown mane of hair. This was not a perfect world. She had never known any bank managers.

'Do you want me to put in a request for the money or not, Miss Howard?' he said sharply. No groping for her name this time, she noticed. Her indignation had rattled him that much at least. It was not much of a victory but it was something.

The shuffling feet behind her were beginning to sound like the percussion section of an orchestra.

'Oh, very well,' she said.

'Then fill out this form. And this.'

'*More* forms? But I've already...'

He was back in control. He smirked. 'We have to check. It is in your own interest. It—' He stopped under her withering stare.

'Don't tell me,' Christina said drily. 'It's the rules. OK, then. Give me the beastly form.'

He gave her two. She bent to fill them out, scribbling with swift efficiency. The woman behind her sighed in resignation, but the clerk looked briefly impressed at the speed with which Christina completed the task.

'Thank you,' he said.

He took them back, applied stamps of various sorts to every conceivable space and handed her back a small sliver of paper with two—or was it three?—stamps on it.

'Come back tomorrow.'

Christina surveyed him cynically.

'You must think I'm a fool. If you're going through this rigmarole, the money won't be here inside a week.'

He had the grace to blush. But he shrugged again. 'You never know.'

'Oh, I know,' Christina said bitterly. 'I've met bureaucrats before.'

Hurriedly he pushed some more paper at her. These looked like brochures of some sort. She picked them up absently, still glaring at him.

He tried a winning smile. 'You could always transfer your account to this branch.'

Christina gave him an incredulous look. His smile faltered. He shuffled papers importantly and tried to sound efficient. 'Yes, well, we'll contact you when your money comes through, Miss Howard.'

'You won't,' she said positively.

He looked affronted. 'I assure you—'

'You won't be able to. If you'd read one of those eighteen forms you've just made me fill out in triplicate, you'd see I haven't got an address in Athens yet,' she pointed out. 'So I'll contact you.'

'I look forward to it,' he said with patent untruth.

Christina did not deign to reply. She turned away from the counter. The queue came to life again. The woman behind her went up to the glass barrier but the clerk was still looking after the long-legged English girl with the fly-away, sun-streaked hair and the Mediterranean tan.

'Oh, Miss Howard,' he called.

Christina turned. Another form? But no. He had remembered his courtesy code, at last.

'Have a nice day.'

'Grr,' said Christina.

She stormed out of the bank.

In fact she stormed so comprehensively that she let the revolving door swing hard, almost into the face of the man following her. The polite official accompanying him leaped to field the door. He looked shocked.

The man's eyes, however, contemplated the departing Christina with amused appreciation. Both men had witnessed the end of her altercation with the clerk.

'Monsieur!' exclaimed the official. He was clearly anxious to defuse the honoured customer's justified indignation.

But the honoured customer was not paying attention. He was still looking after the slim figure storming through the crowd. His expression was a curious mixture of appreciation and regret. The official, who had known him a long time, felt a twinge of sympathy. He wiped all expression from his face, however, and bowed his customer through the door.

Christina was oblivious as she steamed out into the diamond-hard light of an Athenian morning. She was furious.

The money was hers, not the bank's. It represented hours of hard work, sometimes backbreaking work. She was proud of that. And now the bank would not let her get at it! She went to the edge of the pavement and stared across the gleaming, steaming, evil-smelling ribbon of metal and fumes that was Athens's morning traffic jam. The fine temper which had sustained her so far drained away abruptly. If she admitted it, Christina thought wryly, she was as much worried as angry.

The honoured customer, strolling out of the bank, caught sight of Christina hesitating on the pavement. On the point of summoning a car, his hand fell. He looked at her tense figure quizzically.

Christina remained unaware. She pushed the soft, straight hair back from her brow with fingers which shook a little. The man saw that tell-tale tremor. His eyes sharpened.

He hesitated for a moment. Then, with a shrug, he strolled across to her.

'Are you all right?'

Christina jumped at the voice. The words were pleasant enough but the tone was impatient. She turned, her brown hair swinging.

She found that she was being addressed by a tall man in an immaculate biscuit-coloured suit. She did not know anyone who wore suits of that faultless cut. Or who spoke to her with that abrupt harshness, as if in spite of himself.

'What?' she asked blankly.

The man raised an eyebrow, unsmiling. 'You seem a little agitated.'

He was definitely a stranger. From his quick, impatient tones, he seemed as if he could hardly wait to get away from her. And yet... Christina took off her sunglasses the better to see him in the dense shadow of the building behind them. She scanned him candidly.

It was a powerful face rather than a handsome one. He was taller than Christina, who counted herself a tall woman. He was so dark that his skin was almost swarthy. His hair was equally dark. In the brilliant morning it looked black, springing back from a wide, proud brow. Added to that was a strong, imperious nose, a firm jaw, a sculpted mouth in which discipline warred with sensuality, and steeply lidded, sleepy eyes.

He was a seriously sexy man, Christina thought. The attraction blasted out at her like heat from the open door of a furnace. For a moment it took her breath away.

Christina was startled. She did not normally think in those terms. In fact, though she had been good friends with a number of men in the last six years, she could not remember her first reaction to one ever being that little jump of the pulses that acknowledged his masculinity. It immediately made her feel feminine and, somehow, vulnerable.

Her cornflower-blue eyes widened. The thought was not a welcome one. Vulnerability meant weakness, and Christina was not weak. She had worked very hard to win strength and independence and, as she was of her bank balance, she was proud of it.

'Agitated?' she echoed faintly.

He smiled suddenly. It was a dazzling smile.

'Well, you nearly ruined my Roman profile with the revolving door back there,' he told her. He indicated the fashionable offices of the bank they had both just left.

Christina jumped. She even blushed faintly. 'I'm sorry. I didn't realize. I mean, I didn't see you.'

She was floundering under his gaze. Now she came to look at him, she saw that he did not look impatient at all. He looked sleepy—and appreciative. She pulled herself together.

'I was a bit preoccupied,' she admitted, trying to sound cool and unmoved. 'They said I couldn't have my own money. I'm afraid I lost my temper.'

The man gave a soft laugh. 'I saw. Or, at least, I caught the end of it. You seem to have justification.'

Christina was rueful. 'Justification possibly, but I am sure I would have done better to keep my temper. After I started banging the counter that man lost any faint interest he might have had in helping me.'

The man's mouth twitched. 'Understandable,' he murmured.

Christina raised her shoulders in an impatient shrug. 'Yes, I suppose so. Doesn't help me, though. The bank will make damn sure that the whole beastly, bureaucratic process takes as long as possible now. I could see it in that clerk's eyes.'

The man smiled again. It packed a charge, that smile, Christina thought, startled. She blinked.

'Maybe he just wanted to make sure you keep coming back,' he suggested. 'You certainly brighten the place up.'

Christina shook her head. She was feeling a little dazed.

She said in some confusion. 'Oh, I don't think so. He just thought I was being unreasonable.'

'You were,' he told her with brutal frankness. 'The clerk behind the counter doesn't make the rules, you know.'

Christina sniffed. 'He didn't have to gloat over hitting me with them.'

The stranger looked amused. 'How do you know he was gloating? Perhaps he was just embarrassed.'

'He didn't look embarrassed.'

He raised his brows. 'No, maybe not. He has his dignity to consider. But, believe me—' his voice was full of irony '—the last thing a man wants to do is to say no to a beautiful woman. It goes against nature.'

Christina blinked. Beautiful? The compliment was faintly challenging. She met his eyes, bewildered, and saw that they were dancing.

Hurriedly she said, 'I needn't have shouted, I suppose. Anyway I've paid for my bad temper. It means I now have twenty dollars to last me the week.'

This time the man's brows hit his hairline. 'Good grief.'

Christina gave a sudden laugh. It was a warm, bubbly laugh and it was infectious. A woman passing with a small child sent her a harassed smile in response. But the stranger did not smile. Instead his eyes narrowed. For a moment the handsome face was completely blank.

'Can you survive on that?' he asked, shooting the question at her like an accusation.

Christina shrugged. 'I don't know,' she said frankly.

He seemed to take a decision.

'I want to know more about this. I will buy you a coffee while we discuss it.'

Christina did hesitate at that. She looked at him assessingly. In spite of his invitation, in spite of the blazing charm of his smile, she had the sense that he was behaving out of character, and that he was, at some level, almost angry with himself.

It was oddly reassuring. Not that the stranger looked like a cruising Romeo. If he had, thought Christina, she would not have wasted a minute on him. Even if appearances proved deceptive, she could handle it. She was a modern girl and she could keep the masculine desire for flirtation well under control. Still, desire for coffee warred with her habitual dislike of doing what someone else ordered her to do. Coffee won, but only just.

'Thank you,' she said. She could not disguise her faint annoyance.

He had observed her debate.

'Although you don't usually take coffee with perfect strangers?' His lips twitched suddenly. 'I feel I should thank *you*,' he remarked. 'A salutary experience, believe me. This way, I think.'

He took her by the elbow. It was a light hold, barely more than the touch of his fingertips on her bare arm, but Christina was conscious of it through her whole body. She looked at him sideways, startled. The man seemed unaware of the effect he was having on her. Perhaps it was the effect he had on every woman and he was used to it. That tingle certainly did not seem to be mutual, Christina thought wryly. He looked completely unmoved.

He took her to one of the fashionable cafés that Christina would never normally have gone to on her own. Even when she had plenty of cash in her money belt, she restricted herself to the places where students and young, footloose travellers went. But the man looked as if he had never strayed off the wide boulevards in his life. He had the air of one to whom luxury was commonplace.

Watching him from under her eyelashes, Christina realised how right she had been about his elegance. The light-coloured, lightweight suit was virtually creaseless, in spite of the city battering it must have taken this morning. His shirt looked crisp and fresh and the tie he wore was, from its stained-glass colours, real silk.

Final confirmation, if it were needed, was provided by the waiter. The café was full of smartly dressed women with shiny, exclusive carrier bags and besuited men in groups, clattering sugar spoons and worry beads with equal vigour.

Nevertheless, Christina and her unknown companion were led immediately to the best table under the striped awning. It was close to a small orange tree in a pot, whose perfumed flowers almost succeeded in masking the fumes of combustion engines.

At first Christina thought that this was simply the waiter's professional recognition of a wealthy man. But when he addressed her companion as *'Monsieur'* she realised that he did, indeed, know him.

Her companion seated her, before sitting himself in the comfortable basketwork chair at right angles to her.

He looked up at the waiter and spoke in quick, idiomatic Greek. He did not speak it like a Frenchman. Christina, whose command of the language was still imperfect even after five years of summer jobs in the country, listened with mixed admiration and dudgeon.

The waiter wrote down the order and left with a small bow. She noted it particularly. Waiters at pavement cafés, even on the fashionable boulevards, seldom bowed to their customers. She would have demanded an explanation but there was another matter to be dealt with first.

'How did you know I wanted coffee and croissants?' she demanded as soon as the waiter had gone. 'You didn't ask. I am old enough to do my own ordering, you know.'

The man leaned back in his chair, very much at his ease, one arm resting negligently along the curved basketwork arm. Oh, yes, this was a man to whom comfort was an automatic expectation, unworthy of comment. He looked amused at her belligerence.

'But why should you? It was my pleasure.' His tone was suave. 'You had already said yes to coffee. And I assume, if funds are low, that any sustenance will be welcome.' He flicked a glance at his heavy wrist-watch. 'At this time you will not get a full English breakfast, I'm afraid, even here. And it is too soon for lunch. I thought croissants and pastries would fill the gap acceptably while we discuss what to do next.'

She had to admit that she could not fault his reasoning, or withstand that look of wicked amusement which invited her to share it. But Christina went down fighting.

'If they bring me Greek coffee as sweet as barley sugar, I'll get up and leave,' she threatened.

He laughed aloud then. 'It's a deal.'

But when it came the coffee was filtered Colombian with an aroma that was a sensual experience all on its own. Christina closed her eyes and inhaled a scent of wood smoke, she tasted walnuts and heard the chink of brandy glasses at the end of a cordon bleu meal—and all from the warm fumes that wafted up from the cup between her palms.

She sighed in pure, sensuous appreciation. She opened her eyes and met his glance across the table. The brown eyes were dancing.

'Leaving?' he asked softly.

Christina sighed. 'Coffee is possibly my greatest weakness,' she said in resignation.

His mouth slanted. 'I wish I enjoyed my weaknesses with such abandon.'

For no reason she could think of, Christina found her eyes falling away from his. 'I'll stay,' she said hurriedly.

She thanked the waiter in careful Greek. It made him smile as he placed iced water at her elbow and put a basket of freshly baked croissants wrapped in a linen napkin in the middle of the table. It also, she saw out of the corner of her eyes with some satisfaction, raised her companion's eyebrows.

'So coffee's your greatest weakness. That seems a waste.' He pushed an elegant cream jug and sugar bowl across the table towards her. 'It doesn't leave much opportunity for sin,' he observed softly.

Christina decided that she did not want to explore the implications of that. She pushed the hair back from her brow, running her fingers through the newly washed softness absently.

'Enough,' she said, eyeing him warily.

His smile grew, but he did not answer. It left her feeling slightly uneasy.

She helped herself to cream. He took his own coffee black, she saw, with several spoonfuls of sugar. She raised her brows as the third spoonful went in. He chuckled.

'An old Latin American habit,' he murmured. 'My Brazilian uncle used to say coffee should be black as night, hot as hell and sweet as love.'

'Oh,' said Christina taken aback.

She pushed the sugar bowl away from her hurriedly. Without knowing why it did, she felt the warm blood rising under her tan. She was not normally given to blushing and it annoyed her. She took a cooling sip of the ice-cold water that the waiter had brought with her coffee and struggled to appear unmoved.

'Is that where you come from? Latin America? I thought you were French,' she said, determined to shift him out of dangerous territory into polite conversation.

She suspected that he detected her ploy. His eyes crinkled a little at the corners with what might have been secret laughter, but she could not be sure.

He said gravely, 'Oh, I've got French uncles as well. My ancestry is a complete cocktail. It's a long story. I won't bore you with it.'

So it was not a subject open for conversation. That made Christina even more uneasy, for some reason. She allowed her dissatisfaction to appear.

He hesitated briefly she thought, before adding, 'I suppose I should introduce myself. I am Luc Henri.'

There was an odd, loaded pause. He looked at her expectantly, even challengingly. Christina was surprised. Was she supposed to know his name? It meant nothing to her—except that it was obviously French.

She wondered suddenly if any of the other people in the busy café knew him. She looked round. There had been several covert glances in their direction from the elegantly dressed women shoppers.

They were envious glances, Christina realised now. So she was not the only one to rock back on her heels under the impact of that electric attraction. It was a small comfort.

She considered him anew. With a little shock, it was borne in on her that her companion had to be the most attractive man she had ever seen. Certainly he was the most attractive man in the café by a fair margin.

She said slowly. 'Luc Henri? Should that mean something to me?'

The sleepy eyes laughed at her. 'I hope not.'

That startled her. 'What? Why?'

He leaned back in the chair, the morning light glinting on the blue-black hair, turning it into the sleek pelt of a jaguar. It also glinted, Christina saw wryly, on the heavy watch, which was probably gold, and the discreet cuff-links which certainly were. His mouth curved as he looked at her.

'It is a rare experience to talk to a woman whose greatest weakness is coffee,' he said smoothly. 'I think we should keep this encounter of ours out of space and time. Then it can retain its rarity.'

Christina put her head on one side.

'You mean we won't meet again so we can afford to be honest with each other?' she interpreted.

He looked startled. 'You're very acute.'

She gave a bubbling laugh. It made his lips twitch responsively.

'I just like to know where I stand.' She put her elbows on the table and steepled her hands, propping her chin on them while she considered him. 'Of course, I could tell you a complete fantasy. You would never know.'

Luc Henri looked entertained. 'Are you going to?'

Christina looked mischievous. 'It's a temptation,' she admitted. She let her blue eyes go dreamy. 'I could be— oh, a coffee planter's daughter.'

He put back his head and laughed aloud at that. It was a deep, warm sound, like a cello. It seemed to set up some deep echo in Christina. She tingled with it. It was not unpleasant but it gave her an unexpected sense of danger, as if she had walked round an ordinary corner and found herself standing on a precipice.

Startled, she sat upright and stopped playing a game she did not understand.

'On second thoughts, it's probably better not to get carried away,' she said wryly. 'I'm Christina Howard.'

She extended her hand briskly across the table. Luc Henri took it and, to her astonishment, turned it over and inspected its ringless state. His fingers were long and cool. Christina gave a little private shiver at his touch.

Fortunately he did not seem to notice. He shook her hand equally briskly and returned it to her.

'And what are you doing in Greece, Miss Howard? Apart from waiting for funds, of course.'

She acknowledged the dry comment with a smile. She sipped her coffee.

'A tourist?' he prompted.

Christina was affronted. Her Greek was not that bad. 'Of course not. I work.'

There was a small pause while he surveyed her. An odd little smile played about his mouth. 'I see I have offended you. Should I apologise?'

He did not look as if he often apologised, Christina thought. She did not say it. She did not have to. Luc Henri laughed softly.

'There are so many of the young, beautiful and in-digent in Athens. All students who think they can live on air and the classics while they see the sights of Ancient Greece. You seemed to qualify.'

Their eyes met. Christina had the sudden sensation that the precipice had begun to fall away under her feet. And he had called her beautiful again!

She said breathlessly, 'I'm not such a fool.'

He looked sceptical.

She insisted, 'I'm not. I'm short of money because my bank has messed things up, nothing more. I'm not a student. I'm a practical woman. I've never tried to live on air and—and whatever it was in my life.'

'The classics,' he murmured.

His eyes were crinkling up at the corners most decidedly now. He looked as if he was enjoying himself. 'I apologise. What do you—er—work at?'

Christina grinned suddenly. 'I'm a deckhand.'

That shook him as it was intended to do. He blinked.

'A—?' He shook his head and took a mouthful of his coffee. Then he shook his head again. 'It's no good. I thought you said a deckhand.'

'I did.'

His jaw did not quite drop but the blank look on his face was rewarding. Well pleased with this reaction, Christina helped herself to a buttery croissant, pulled the corner off and chewed with enjoyment.

'But—why?'

'Now that's as long a story as your ancestry,' she said demurely.

The dark face showed brief incredulity, as if he was not used to being denied what he wanted to know. His brows twitched together. 'Are you suggesting a trade, Christina Howard?'

She looked innocent. He was not deceived.

'My family tree for your extraordinary career choice?'

'Well, I don't tell people normally. And you obviously don't talk about your family,' she pointed out.

He seemed amused—suddenly, deeply amused. 'So it would be a fair trade? Well, I see your point. And certainly I don't normally talk about my family. You are quite right about that.'

His shoulders shook a little. Christina's faint suspicions grew.

'Are you sure I shouldn't know you?' she demanded.

He shook his head, his eyes brimming with that private laughter.

'Then—'

'Your career,' he interrupted firmly. 'Tell.'

Christina set her jaw. 'You first. You might chicken out.'

'O ye of little faith,' he mourned. But his mouth still looked as if he was laughing inside. 'Very well. My mother was French. My grandfather was a mad explorer and he dragged his family along with him wherever he went. My aunt Monique married a Brazilian tennis player who lived half his life in the jungle with remote Indian tribes. Very dashing and just possibly a touch madder than my grandfather. At least, that's what my father used to say.'

'And what is he—your father I mean?'

A brief sadness touched his face. 'Was, I'm afraid.'

'I'm sorry,' murmured Christina.

It was clear that he had liked his father.

'Was he an explorer too?'

'No.' He seemed to bring himself back out of the past. 'No, he was more of—well, you would call him an administrator, I suppose.'

'Civil servant,' interpreted Christina.

Luc Henri looked startled. Then his lips twitched. 'You could call him that, certainly.'

'And you? Explorer or civil servant? Or neither?'

'That wasn't in the bargain,' he protested. But he answered readily enough. 'Civil servant, definitely. Explorers have horribly uncomfortable lives. I like to be comfortable.'

But there was something about the way he said it—to say nothing of the broad set of his muscular shoulders—that made Christina suspect that she was being teased again. She was not sure she liked it.

He turned compelling eyes on her. 'And you? How did you become a deckhand?'

'Oh, that's easy. It was a bid for freedom.'

He looked astonished. 'I have heard much about sailing but I've never heard that anyone but the owner of the boat had much freedom.'

Christina looked at him with new respect. 'You're right there,' she agreed.

'But it was still freedom for you? Were you escaping from a convent?'

She shook her head, laughing. 'Very nearly. A polite girls' school. Have you ever been to one?'

His eyes danced. 'I'm afraid not.'

'Don't be afraid. It's not an experience to be envied.'

'If it was so bad why didn't your parents take you away?'

'Parent,' Christina corrected him swiftly. 'She thought I was jolly lucky getting a scholarship to a school where the girls passed lots of exams. She could never have afforded to send me there without it. And I didn't tell her. Anyway it wasn't bad. Just boring.'

'More boring than a deckhand's life?' he asked, a cynical note in his voice.

Christina gave him a straight look. 'Deckhands travel. Until I came out here all the travelling I ever did was the journey to and from school.' She took another mouthful of croissant. 'But school was a long time ago.'

'Not that long,' he said drily.

Christina shook her head. 'Don't be deceived,' she said calmly. 'I'm older than I look.'

'That's just as well. You look about twelve at the moment,' he said.

He leaned forward and brushed a flake of sweet pastry from her chin. Christina choked. He sat back, his eyes glinting.

'There. Back with the adults again.'

She was blushing. 'Thank you. Very kind of you,' she said furiously, not meaning a word of it.

He did not pretend to misunderstand. He laughed. 'My pleasure. So you ran away to sea twenty years ago. How have you lived since then?'

Christina sniffed. 'I earn a decent living.' She scowled at the sweet roll in her hand. 'At least, I do when the bank lets me get at my money.'

Luc Henri shook his head. 'Who on earth is mad enough to employ a girl like you as a deckhand?'

'I'm perfectly competent,' she flung at him, annoyed.

His eyes caught and held hers. He had extraordinary eyelashes, she saw now—thick and dark, defining those brilliant eyes like a painter's charcoal line.

'And perfectly beautiful,' he returned softly.

Christina caught her breath. Again! She stiffened slightly. Her eyes slid away from his.

'You should see me in my working clothes,' she said, her voice a little strained.

'I am imagining it.' His voice was dry. 'I'd be amazed if the rest of the crew do any work at all.'

Christina sat even straighter. 'I don't have affairs with colleagues,' she said bluntly.

He looked amused. 'Then who do you have affairs with?'

'I don't—' she began heatedly and stopped herself at once, but it was too late. She had given herself away. He made no attempt to hide his triumph. His eyes gleamed with it.

'Don't you? I find that very interesting.'

Christina fought down a blush and regarded him with exasperation. 'If you say I ought to, a beautiful girl like me, I shall scream,' she told him.

His lips twitched. 'I'm not that unsubtle.'

'You surprise me,' she said sarcastically.

Luc Henri's slim brows lifted. 'Because I pay you compliments you're not used to?'

'How do you know—?' She bit the sentence off—too late again. This time she was furious with herself.

The look he gave her was almost tender.

'Women who are used to receiving compliments don't ignore them,' he explained kindly. 'You aren't and you do. At least you try to. How old are you, Christina?'

'Twenty-three,' she flung at him.

He smiled. 'You surprise me,' he mimicked.

Christina ground her teeth.

'Now tell me about these boats you work on.'

Christina tossed her head. 'Private yachts mostly. Or tourist boats taking people scuba-diving. I'm good. I can get as much work as I want.'

'And you earn enough to keep yourself?'

She gave her bubbling laugh suddenly. 'When the bank lets me get at it.'

He looked at her curiously. 'But surely it's seasonal? What do you do in the winter?'

Christina gave a small, private smile. Here was an opportunity to get some of her own back at last. 'That's my business.'

She found that he was watching her, a frown between his brows. He did not seem to have noticed that she had balked him. He looked as if he was in a quandary—and that he was not going to tell her about it.

'You're an odd girl,' he said abruptly.

'Woman,' she corrected him.

His mouth twisted suddenly. 'An even odder woman. I wonder—? No.'

She was not going to ask. She was not even going to think of asking.

She took a mouthful of croissant. 'Not that odd,' she said calmly. 'I work, I eat, I sleep like everyone else.'

The steeply lidded eyes lifted. 'How wrong you are,' he said quietly. 'Not like anyone else I've ever known.'

It was not said provocatively but Christina straightened sharply. Her eyes locked with his. Challenge sizzled in the air between them. Luc went very still.

After a long moment she said, almost at random, 'You don't know me.'

His eyes still held hers. 'Do I not?'

She shivered suddenly. *'No.'* Her voice was sharp. 'No, you don't. This is an encounter out of space and time. Remember?'

He said softly, 'You're scared of me, Christina.'

'Don't be ridiculous. Of course I'm not. I can take care of myself. I'm not scared of you or anyone.'

Luc looked at her for a moment. 'If you're not scared of me, what does scare you?'

She seized another mouthful of croissant and chewed it, avoiding his eyes. 'I told you, I'm not scared.'

'Then why won't you look at me?'

Christina choked. 'You're imagining it.' She met his eyes with a candour which cost her a lot of self-control. 'Look, I'm not scared of being alone in the city with nowhere to stay tonight. What makes you more scary than that?'

There was an odd look in his eyes. 'You tell me.'

'You're imagining it,' Christina said again, too loudly.

Several of the other customers looked up, startled. The man at the next table was so surprised that he knocked over his glass of water. He dropped his *Wall Street Journal* and the liquid began to soak into it. He looked wretchedly uncomfortable as the waiter ran to mop the table.

Christina, who had been aware of the man's gaze on them for some time, was not displeased. 'Now he'll have to find something else to pretend to do while he eavesdrops,' she said.

Luc Henri's eyes passed over the dark-suited, middle-aged man without interest.

'Eavesdrops? I think you must be mistaken. He's probably waiting for someone.'

She shook her head.

'No. He came in not long after us and chose this table deliberately. He's just been pretending to read that newspaper. He didn't turn the pages once.'

A shade of annoyance crossed Luc Henri's face. But all he said was, 'Then he can't have had a very entertaining morning.'

He looked at his watch, then raised a finger at the waiter for the bill.

'Thank you for my breakfast,' Christina said at once, retreating into formal manners. 'I ought to be going.'

At once he said imperiously, 'No.'

She paused, one eyebrow raised at his tone.

He smiled faintly. 'At least let me lend you some money to cover tonight's lodging.'

Christina looked at him levelly. 'Lend? You mean give, don't you, if we're not going to meet again?'

Luc stared at her, his brows twitching together. He said something explosive under his breath. It did not sound polite. 'I can afford it.'

'Ah, but can I?' she retorted.

His look was quizzical suddenly. 'No strings.'

Christina's heart missed a beat. She shook her head decisively. 'Thank you, no. I should be able to crash on someone's floor tonight. It won't take long to get a job. I'll ask around the waterfront cafés tonight.'

He said quickly, 'Think of me as a brother. I would hope someone would do as much for my sister—or my niece when she's older.'

Christina looked at him levelly. 'I don't feel like your sister. Or your niece.'

A little flame leaped into his eyes. She saw that she had made a mistake. She pushed her coffee-cup away from her and stood up quickly.

'I'm grateful for the offer, truly I am. But when I set out on my own I promised myself I'd pay my bills as I went. I always do. So, thank you, but no.' She held out her hand. 'It's been interesting meeting you. Have a nice life.'

He stood up as well. His face was thunderous suddenly. If she had been his employee she would have quailed at that expression, she thought. She was grateful that she did not work for him.

Luc's face darkened. He flicked open his wallet and pulled out a thick sandwich of notes.

'Don't be stupid,' he said curtly. 'Take the money.'

The man at the next table did not know where to look. Out of the corner of her eye Christina caught his expression—half wretchedly embarrassed, half fascinated. She found that she sympathised with him. Luc Henri clearly was sublimely unaware of the scene he was making, or did not care what people thought of him. In contrast, the poor man at the next table was acutely aware of both. It made her all the more furious with Luc Henri.

She leaned forward across the table, glaring. 'Try listening. I am not your sister,' she hissed.

'If you were I would have drilled some sense into you by now,' Luc Henri flung back between his teeth. He was clearly in a right royal rage and saw no reason to curb his temper.

'You don't surprise me in the least,' Christina said with poisonous sweetness. '"Sense" being anything that agrees with you, I take it?'

He drew an angry breath. Then, even as she watched him, she saw him catch hold of his retort and wrestle it down like a man struggling with a wild animal. He closed his lips tight on whatever it was he had been going to say.

'You are an education, Miss Howard. My powers of argument seem to be deserting me,' he said thinly at last. 'Please be sensible...'

Christina stood her ground. 'Don't patronise me,' she said quietly.

They stood sizing each other up over the table like duellists. Then he smiled. It was not one of his dazzling smiles. It was more like an insult.

'You needn't worry that I'd expect payment in kind,' Luc Henri drawled. 'Women come to me of their own free will.'

The man at the next table gasped. So did Christina. She felt her face flame. It did not sweeten her temper one iota. But it made her forget briefly that they were in a public place and that, unlike her arrogant opponent, she minded making a spectacle of herself. The anger coursed through her like a forest fire, but she wiped the expression off her face and gave him her most demure smile.

Leaning forward, she twitched the notes out of his hand. The man at the next table shuddered and backed his chair away with a scream of steel-tipped legs across the concrete.

Luc Henri's eyes had narrowed to slits.

'Not me,' Christina said gently.

The narrowed eyes dared her, blatantly. Christina smiled. She stepped back and, with a quick little movement, tossed the notes high, high up into the air.

They were still falling on the startled patrons as she threaded her way between the tables and left.

CHAPTER TWO

CHRISTINA plunged along the street, her heart beating furiously. How dared he? Oh, how *dared* he? Interfering! Ordering her around! Lecturing her as if he were the head of the family and she a tiresome teenager! Pressing his money on her as if she were some scatterbrain who did not know where she was going to sleep tonight! As if he had the *right*!

Here her outraged musings brought her up short. The interfering Mr Luc Henri might not have any right to lecture her but there was no doubt that in one way he was right. She had not got anywhere to stay tonight. Christina grinned suddenly. She would end up on a bench in the bus station if she did not start making some calls right now.

In spite of Luc Henri's patent scepticism, it was not difficult. Christina was a girl who took friendship seriously and people responded in kind.

Sue Stanley was waiting, the door already open by the time Christina arrived at the top of the steep stairs to her studio. They hugged. She yawned widely.

'Oh, hell,' said Christina in quick comprehension. 'Night shift last night?'

She was a nurse. She nodded and led the way inside.

'I'm sorry.' Christina was remorseful. 'I didn't mean to get you out of bed.'

Sue chuckled. 'Somebody has to. Mr Right still hasn't put in an appearance.' She hefted Christina's bag squashily onto a rough wooden chair and led the way to the small kitchen. 'What about you?'

Christina made a face. Her mother had spent half her life waiting for Mr Right to come and rescue her from the problems of everyday life. Meanwhile it had been her young daughter who had tried to manage their disorganised life, until her mother had died. The experience had given Christina a strong distaste even for joking about that mythical beast.

Sue knew her very well. She grinned. 'No guy made a dint in the armour yet?'

'And not likely to.'

Sue shook her head. 'You'll find out one day,' she prophesied.

For no reason at all that she could think of, Luc Henri's imperious face slipped into Christina's mind. She remembered that odd, intent look in his eyes. Involuntarily she shivered a little. It was not an unpleasurable shiver.

That startled her. Luc Henri had nothing to do with her, she reminded herself. She would never see him again. She did not even *want* to see him again. Did she?

She said with less than her usual calm, 'That's nonsense and you know it.'

The balcony was a blaze of coral and scarlet geraniums in terracotta tubs. Sue led the way outside. Christina sank down onto the top step of the fire escape and looked round with pleasure.

She found Sue was looking at her measuringly. 'Who is he?'

Christina stiffened faintly. 'Who is who?'

She had first worked with Christina three years before on a boat attached to an archaeological expedition. All through the summer they had shared their confidences, their crises and their nail scissors. As a result they knew each other very well.

Now Sue was looking at her shrewdly. 'Whoever kicked you out this morning.'

Christina relaxed again. 'You're on the wrong track, Sue. I came off a boat, that's all. Then I found the bank wouldn't let me have any cash until the weekend.'

She stared. 'You? But you're always so efficient about money.'

'The bank seems to be less so—some administrative hitch,' Christina said drily.

Sue could believe it, though she was less convinced that a man was not the cause of Christina's present predicament. She said so.

To her own, furious incomprehension, Christina blushed. Sue did not even pretend not to notice. 'I knew it,' she said gleefully. 'Tell me, what's he like?'

'You're not exactly tactful,' Christina complained.

Which of course convinced Sue that her deductions were correct. 'Oh, tact,' she said dismissively. 'No fun in that. Tell me about this dangerous heartthrob of yours.'

In spite of herself Christina laughed. 'Why would he be dangerous?'

'If he wasn't dangerous, you wouldn't notice him,' Sue told her with brutal honesty.

Christina was a little shocked. Disturbed too at how well Sue seemed to know her.

'What do you mean?'

Her friend sighed. 'Chris, I've seen it too often. Most of the time you just don't seem to *notice*. Strong men paw the ground with lust and you treat them like brothers. Or another girlfriend.'

Christina was moved to protest. 'Nonsense.'

'It isn't, you know. A man is only going to get you to notice him if he picks you up by your pigtails and hauls you off to his lair.' She sighed. 'You'll get it too.' She sounded envious.

It did not amuse Christina. Sue saw it and, good friend that she was, stopped teasing.

'Nothing to do with me if you like your men dangerous. Anyway, I can't sit out here in the sun all day. I've got to get to the market before all the decent vegetables go. Make yourself at home.'

She went. She left Christina restless and uneasy.

Was Sue right? And if so, why had she never said it before? Had the encounter with Luc Henri, brief as it had been, awakened something dormant in Christina which Sue, who knew her so well, recognised? It was not a palatable thought.

It had to be nonsense, of course. He was a high-handed man who was used to having his own way. She hardly knew him. What she did know she didn't like. It was a relief to know that she was highly unlikely to meet him again. And yet...

There had been *something*, hadn't there? Something between them, tense but unspoken. Something she had never felt before. It had made her tingle when he'd looked at her, so that she'd been aware of him to her bones. Christina's mouth dried as she thought about it.

This would never do. Life had to be managed. It was no good letting yourself be distracted by fantasies of a man you did not even know.

She armed herself with a pen and her address book, installed herself at the pay-phone in the dark little hall and began the business of managing her life again. Nobody offered her a job on the spot but she got enough tentative interest to restore her spirits. It almost succeeded in banishing Luc Henri's disturbing image.

When Sue came back with her purchases the evening breeze was beginning to stir the hot city air. Christina was on the balcony. She had pulled on a cotton top and her long, bare legs were already turning to their habitual summer gold. Sue came to the French window and looked down at her.

'You look wonderful.' She sighed, flopping onto the sill. 'I *wish* I was a natural blonde with legs to my eyebrows.'

Christina scrambled up. 'No, you don't. It wouldn't go with your wardrobe. Coffee?'

'I'd sell what's left of my soul for some.'

'You've got it.'

She went inside and busied herself with the ancient percolator.

Sue called out, 'Any luck with jobs?'

'There's a four-day tour to Ancient Sites that needs a guide. Not really my scene but if I can't get anything else . . .'

'Did that take all day?'

Christina took Sue's coffee out to her and sank onto the fire escape, cross-legged.

'No. I did a few sketches.'

'The Christina beachwear collection?'

The teasing was affectionate. Sue knew all about Christina's Italian course in design and how seriously she took it. She worked at it in the winter, using the proceeds of her summer jobs to pay the substantial fees and her modest living costs.

Now Christina grinned. 'Maybe. The sun out here is certainly inspirational.'

Sue stretched. 'Mmm. I love this place. With sun like this who needs to work?'

'Those who like to eat,' said Christina prosaically. 'Speaking of which, I ought to go down to the harbour tonight. I might pick up a job from one of the captains.'

She looked at Sue apologetically. They both knew that that was where masters looking for crews were likely to be found. Yet it seemed rude to go out and leave her friend the first night she was staying with her. Sue read her mind easily. She grinned at her over the rim of the mug.

'Fine. I'll even come with you. As long as you're not on your own, the harbour's fun. I can do with some fun to set me up for my next stint at the hospital.' She stretched again. 'I need to shower and change. Then, look out, Athens.'

They did not get to the harbour area till ten. The night was clear but crisp this early in the season. A few of the fiercer stars shone through in spite of the competition from neon streetlighting and the smog bubble engendered by the city. The cafés were loud with talk and recorded music. The smell of barbecued meat, garlic, wine and humanity filled the dusty streets.

'Mmm,' said Christina with pleasure. 'Costa's first, I think. Lots of the captains hang out there. Aldo Marino may be looking for a crew, Jackie said.'

Christina was well-known in Costa's busy little café. As they threaded their way between the wooden tables, several of the diners raised a hand in greeting. Costa himself interrupted his work to greet Christina with a smacking kiss.

'Aldo? Don't think so,' Costa told them. He went back to shovelling Greek salad busily into individual bowls without stopping. 'There's always Demetrius.' He nodded in the direction of a morose-looking man at a corner table. 'If you're desperate,' he added frankly.

'You're not that desperate,' Sue said firmly. 'The man's a cheapskate. Skimps on everything.'

At the back of the café a bouzouki player was looking at Christina with undisguised appreciation. He flashed her a brilliant smile and began to sing a love song with distinctly suggestive lyrics. Christina laughed at his bold eyes but she shook her head.

It was not like the way Luc Henri had looked at her, she thought involuntarily: that had turned her still and watchful, had caused some small, cold excitement to unfold. The bouzouki player was never going to be able to make her blush in a month of Sundays. Luc had done it with a word.

What's happening to me? she thought, startled. Do I take the man with me everywhere I go?

Sue plucked at her arm. 'Come on. Let's try the Blue Taverna.'

Recalled to the present, Christina jumped. 'Oh, OK.'

'Good evening,' said a soft voice.

Christina whirled, her heart pounding as if a deadly enemy had suddenly caught up with her. Luc Henri was standing there studying her. A small smile curled the handsome mouth. It was another of those smiles that did not reach his arrogant eyes.

Christina's heart sank like an anchor in still water. She had not the slightest idea why. She straightened her shoulders and tried to pretend that she did not care.

'Oh,' she said. 'You.'

He gave a little bow.

From the far side of the room, a cheerful Australian voice called, 'Sue. Where've you been hiding? Over here, gorgeous.'

'Geoff,' said Sue. She hesitated, took in the quiet elegance of Luc Henri's appearance, and decided that Christina did not need a chaperon with such an eminently respectable personage. 'I'll see you at the flat,' she muttered, and disappeared among the crowded tables.

Christina, who had never in her life thought that she needed a chaperon, felt suddenly, alarmingly alone. The friendly crowd and the noise somehow made it worse. She swallowed.

Luc Henri was looking at her with a cynical expression that she did not like at all. He did not speak. Christina cleared her throat.

'Time and place seem to have caught up with us, then,' she said flippantly. 'What are you doing at Costa's?'

'I could ask the same. Except that it's obvious.'

His tone was pleasant enough. There was nothing she could take exception to in the words themselves. So how did she know that he was insulting her, and that he was coldly, furiously angry? Was it the cold glitter of his eyes? Christina glanced round. No one else showed any signs of noticing anything untoward. In fact, no one else was paying any attention to them at all.

'I'm sorry, I don't understand,' she said.

He gave a bark of laughter. It did not sound amused.

'Cruising. Isn't that what they call it?'

Christina's brows knitted. 'What?'

He made an angry gesture with his hand, embracing the whole café—the bouzouki player, Costa's beefy geniality and even the harassed waiters.

'You make the most of your natural assets, I'll say that for you. A smile, a lot of long, bare leg and the odd promise of a kiss. It's a potent inducement, even if I can see that. Is that what you meant when you said you could look after yourself?'

For a moment Christina was so stunned that she did not think she was understanding him properly. When she realised that he meant exactly what she thought he meant, she went white with temper.

'I think you're calling me a tart.'

He gave that harsh laugh again. 'Oh, no. I respect tarts. They're honest working women in their way.'

'What the hell do you mean by that?'

His eyes looked her up and down in a brief, insulting flick which considered and then dismissed her. She took a step backwards as if he had hit her. Her face flamed. He saw it and smiled.

'I mean that they deliver what they contract for,' he drawled. 'Or so I'm told. Whereas you—' He shook his head. 'No, no, my dear.'

Christina took a hasty step towards him. His derisive smile grew.

'Thinking of slapping my face? You couldn't do it, you know. You're much too nicely brought up.'

'You know nothing at all about how I was brought up.'

'Oh, I think you're wrong there.' He put his head on one side and pretended to consider. 'I know the signs. I can't think how I missed them this morning.'

She was trembling with anger. 'What signs?'

'Lovely manners. Minimal morals,' he said succinctly.

They might have been alone. Christina was hardly aware of the crowded café. Neither of them had raised their voice but their argument was too intense to escape attention. They were beginning to attract the occasional sideways look, but she did not notice that either. She could not remember ever being so angry in her life.

'What right have you got to talk about my morals?'

'Right?' He shrugged. 'None.'

'Or to sit in judgement on me on the basis of ten minutes' spying? Or was it as much as that? I didn't see you when we came in. Maybe you've only just arrived. Maybe we're talking about ten seconds' spying here.'

'Call it five minutes,' Luc Henri said negligently.

'Well, then—'

'Five memorable minutes.'

Christina stared.

'I watched. Fascinating. You kissed the owner. Well, I suppose ownership of a waterfront café brings some perks.'

Christina gasped but Luc did not appear to notice. He swept on, itemising her actions with precision, and putting the worst possible gloss on them.

'You swung what passes for a skirt at the group at the corner table. And it only took one bat of your eyelashes at the boy who plays that noisy substitute for a guitar to gain his devoted attention.'

She was so angry that she did not even think of defending herself. In fact, after a brief moment of blank outrage, she decided to prove to him that she was every bit as bad as he thought her—and worse. So she gave a careless laugh and shrugged. Her crocheted top slipped off one bare brown shoulder.

Christina felt rather than saw his eyes follow the falling fabric. He could not repress his reaction and it was not disapproval. She registered it with a glow of something like triumph.

It was utterly unlike her. Anger must have made her reckless, she thought. Resisting the instinct to pull the top back into place, she shook back her hair and lifted her chin defiantly. She met his eyes with a look quite as contemptuous as his own.

'So?' she said softly. 'What business is it of yours?'

For a moment he did not answer. Then he looked deliberately at the sagging top. 'So you like to play with fire,' he mused. 'Now why didn't I pick that up before?'

Her eyes narrowed to slits. 'I said, What business is it of yours?' Her voice rose.

'Oh, come on, lady. You're not that nicely brought up.'

She knew he was going to reach for her but she still did not quite believe it. Not now, not here, with a crowd of evening diners looking on. It was not the sort of thing that happened to her. It was not the sort of thing that ultra-civilised men like Luc Henri did.

There was nothing civilised in the way he jerked her off her feet to bring her hard against him. For a moment he held her breast to breast, looking down into her defiant eyes with a curious expression, almost as if behind the anger he was in pain. But the impression of pain was gone in an instant and he was laughing. 'Burn, fire, burn,' he said cynically.

And she was engulfed.

The thought flashed across Christina's mind: well, he is certainly not treating me as if I were his sister now. It was her last coherent thought for some time.

For all the cynicism, he was not playing games. His hands were hard on her slim frame—mercilessly hard. And his mouth was hungry.

The crowded café, the smell of spiced meats and hot bread, the sounds of talk and laughter and wine being poured from rough glass carafes all receded as if they did not exist. Christina's head fell back under the on-slaught of his kiss. Her dazed eyes drifted shut. She felt as if her bones were melting. She had no strength in the powerful circle of his arms, no wish for strength, no resistance at all. All she knew was that her blood was pounding in her veins, driving her deeper and deeper into his embrace. And that she had never felt like this before.

Luc's arms tightened.

He was giving no quarter, she realised dimly. He was so angry that neither the public place nor her blank as-tonishment was holding him back. In fact, she had a faint suspicion that they normally would have done and he knew it; so the fact that this uninhibited sexual demand was out of character was adding fuel to his anger. Of the anger there was no doubt at all. Nor of the demand.

His mouth ravaged the softness of hers until she could hardly breathe. She felt the blood beating frantically at his pulse points, battering at her. She felt his breath in her throat, her lungs. She smelled a faint, unfamiliar, woody scent which seemed to come from his light jacket. It failed entirely to mask the darker, stronger smell from his heated skin. It half repelled her, half fascinated her.

It was a wholly new sensation. It set her trembling even as it made her feel gloriously alive. The relentless kiss relaxed at last. Christina made a small animal noise and turned her head blindly to seek the hollow between his throat and shoulder with her lips.

Luc gave a sharp exclamation. He flinched as if he had burned himself. He pushed her to arm's length almost savagely. Christina swayed and opened her eyes. She blinked. He looked murderous. She could feel the tremor in the hands clamped on her shoulders, holding her away from him. He looked as if he wanted to shake the life out of her.

'That seems to answer your question.' His voice was uneven. He was breathing hard but otherwise the iron self-control was back.

Christina shook her head. She did not recover so quickly.

'Question?' she echoed blankly.

'What business it is of mine,' Luc reminded her. There was an edge to his voice.

Christina stared at him in gathering disbelief. 'Are you saying *that* makes me your business?'

'Of course.'

'You're out of your mind,' she said heatedly.

His mouth quirked. 'Quite possibly.'

She ignored that. 'Just because you have the gall to force yourself upon me... in front of everyone—' She broke off, lost for words.

Instead she looked eloquently round the café. The diners seemed to be making too big a thing of being totally absorbed by their food. Christina was fairly sure that a minute earlier they had been mesmerized by the scene between the tall dark stranger and the English girl they had never seen behave like that before. It made her want to scream with rage.

He said softly, 'I didn't hear you calling for help.'

'What?'

He repeated it. His voice was quiet but his eyes were dangerous.

Christina was not intimidated. She was shaking with justified temper. At least, she told herself it was temper. At his contemptuous words her rage hit boiling point. She stepped back out of his hands.

'Then hear me now,' she said grimly. She turned her head and shouted at the top of her voice, 'Costa!'

Luc winced, but the dangerous glint went out of his eyes. It was replaced by surprise. Then, astoundingly, came amusement and even a hint of admiration. Or so Christina thought, viewing him from behind a red mist of fury.

The proprietor appeared so quickly that she suspected he had been waiting for such a summons. He did not look like a righteously vengeful protector of insulted innocence, however. He looked hugely amused and was not trying very hard to hide it.

'Throw this jerk out,' Christina said in a choked voice.

'I can't do that, Christina.'

She turned astounded eyes on Costa. 'You saw what he did.'

Costa chuckled. 'I'm not a policeman, Christina. As long as the clients pay their bill and don't break the crockery, they can do what they like.' He thought about it. 'They can even break the crockery if they pay for it.'

'What if they offend other clients?' she flashed.

'Don't worry your head about it. They enjoyed it,' Costa said soothingly.

Luc gave a choke of laughter. He suppressed it but not quickly enough.

Christina was outraged. She stamped her foot. She made a noise like Sue's elderly kettle coming to the boil. '*I* didn't enjoy it.'

'Then I'm sorry, of course. But I don't see what you expect me to do about it.'

'Throw him out,' she yelled.

The diners began to look interested again. She subsided, rather flushed.

Costa smiled at her paternally. 'Look at it from my point of view. I can't throw a man out just because you don't think he kisses very well,' he said in a reasonable tone. 'Besides—'

Christina gave him a steely glare. 'Besides?' she prompted dangerously.

He shrugged his beefy shoulders. 'To be honest, my dear, I've seen worse.'

This time Luc did not even try to disguise his laughter. 'Poor Christina. I don't think the US Marines are going to speed to the rescue this trip,' he said when his mirth subsided. He nodded at a table. 'Why don't you sit down? Costa can bring us a bottle of his best ouzo and we'll talk things over.'

Luc and Costa exchanged a look of pure masculine complacency. Christina saw it and recognised an unspoken conspiracy. They thought that she was beaten. She would show them.

Across the café tables Sue was already half out of her seat. Christina bit back her smile. Oh, she would certainly show them. She looked away quickly before Luc could follow her eyes. She had to buy time.

It went against the grain but she said meekly, 'Oh, all right. I have to go to the cloakroom first, though.'

Neither of the men demurred. She met Sue's eyes compellingly and turned deliberately. Out of the corner of her eye she saw Sue murmur an excuse to her companions and follow her.

In the poky little cloakroom Christina ran her wrists under cold water. She peered in the cracked mirror. Her eyes were wide and a little wild. Her skin felt cold and sensitised, as if someone had coated it with ice. Damn that man. Damn him. How dared he make her feel like this? The door opened.

'Wow,' said Sue. 'That was really *something*. I take it he's the "administrative hitch" from this morning?'

Christina glared at her unflattering reflection. 'No, he isn't. And he's not going to be any sort of hitch at all,' she said firmly. 'I'm not having a stranger order me around.'

Sue blinked. 'Have you told him that?'

'Several times.'

Sue gave a gurgle of laughter. 'I thought he didn't look the type to give up easily.'

'Well, he's going to have to learn a new skill,' said Christina with resolution. 'He's not pushing me about any more.'

Sue sighed. 'He could push me about any time he liked.'

Christina turned away from the mirror. 'You wouldn't enjoy it,' she assured her.

'Oh, yes, I would. He's gorgeous. If he looked at me the way he looked at you, I'd just lie down and die for him.'

Christina was startled. 'How he looked at me?'

'I know you usually ignore the effect you have on men but you must have noticed *that*,' Sue said in disgust. 'From the moment you came in, he couldn't take his eyes off you. I thought he was going to *eat* you.'

Christina remembered that devouring kiss. She put up a hand to ease the sudden constriction in her throat.

'So did I,' she said in a low voice. She shivered.

Instantly, Sue was all contrition. 'Sorry. I'm a fool. No matter how gorgeous he looks, if he keeps after you when you've made it clear he doesn't turn you on, he's a heel.' She patted her friend's shoulder. 'Count on me.'

It wasn't that he did not turn her on, exactly... Christina dismissed it. It was too complicated to explain to Sue, especially when she didn't entirely understand it herself. And she certainly wanted to escape from Luc Henri as far and as fast as she could.

'I want to get out of here without him seeing me. And get away before he can follow.'

Sue was thoughtful. 'Hmm. You can't go through the kitchen because Costa's on his side,' she said shrewdly.

Christina looked surprised at her perception.

Sue nodded. 'All that machismo. Costa just loves it. He'd tell. Unless he didn't know.' She paused. 'Dustbins,' she said suddenly.

Sue shot out of the door. Christina stared after her. In less than a minute she was back.

'That yard is dis*gust*ing,' she said with feeling. 'No one would eat here if they saw it. Still, that means no one is going to search it too carefully. Go and lurk behind the cabbage stalks and I'll go and get Geoff. We'll get some transport from somewhere and come and pick you up. Just keep out of sight for ten minutes.'

Christina went. The yard was quite as foul as Sue had said. She held her breath for as long as she could. After that she breathed through her mouth.

There was a commotion in the kitchen behind her but she could not make out whether it was an irate Luc Henri turning the place upside down in search of her or just normal family give and take. She tensed and held her breath with even more resolution than before. Her heart beat faster. Someone opened the door to the yard, muttered a startled imprecation and shut it hurriedly. Christina breathed again.

Sue and Geoff turned up a few moments later. Geoff's amused face appeared over the edge of the wooden fence that surrounded the yard and he reached out a hand.

'Phew. That guy really scared you, didn't he?' he said, hauling her out into the road. 'I wouldn't have spent three minutes in there on a bet. You'll probably start to go mouldy.'

'I'll watch out for it,' Christina assured him solemnly. 'And he did *not* scare me. I just chose not to argue in public any more. Thanks for the help,' she added belatedly.

'Any time. Any friend of Sue's...' he said largely. He sounded entertained. 'What are you going to do now? Get out of town?'

'Don't be silly. He's a civilised man.' She paused and added with a certain amount of relief, 'Anyway, he doesn't know where I'm staying.'

'He could find out. Looks the kind of guy who wouldn't have trouble doing just that.'

Geoff had hired a rickety Citroën. It was parked on the corner of the dark lane, Sue hunched anxiously over the wheel. He opened the passenger door and pulled the front seat forward to let Christina scramble into the back.

'Better crouch,' he advised, still amused.

Christina disposed herself on the cramped back seat with dignity. 'He's not going to send out search parties—' she began.

Sue said sharply. 'Don't be so sure of that. What's that behind us?'

A stretched limousine had come into the driving mirror. They all looked over their shoulders. It had headlamps like searchlights. It was inching along the kerb as if it was looking for something. It looked horribly purposeful.

'Duck,' Geoff said.

Christina abandoned her dignity and flung herself on the floor. Not a moment too soon. Geoff grabbed Sue into a comprehensive embrace, so the headlights of the limousine only illuminated a courting couple totally absorbed in each other. It slowed briefly, then, seemingly satisfied, passed on without stopping. In the grateful darkness, Geoff released Sue.

'Chris,' Sue said in a shaken voice, 'I take it back. You're right. I *wouldn't* enjoy it.' Geoff hugged her comfortingly.

'Changed your mind about getting out of town?' he asked Christina with a hint of steel in his pleasant voice. 'Bearing in mind you're staying with Sue.'

'As soon as I can,' said Christina. The limousine had looked menacing. Suddenly, acting as a tour guide to the classical sites seemed immensely attractive.

'Good,' he said.

Sue did not say anything but her relief was none the less clear for being unspoken. She let the car into gear and began to back into the metalled road.

'What I want to know,' she burst out at last, 'is who the hell is this man?'

'Luc Henri,' said Christina in a small voice.

'I've never heard of him.'

'No—well, nor have I.'

'That limo did not belong to the sort of man we've never heard of,' Geoff said.

Christina bit her lip. She remembered that challenging look Luc had given her when he told her his name. Should she have recognised him? Was it a false name? It was an oddly chilling thought.

'What do you think?' she asked Geoff.

'Well, that car belongs to someone powerful. Or someone whose job takes him among the powerful. I got a good look at him in the café. I didn't recognise him. So I'd say he's either a security guard or a businessman.'

Sue said suddenly, 'Whatever he is, he wants you. I wouldn't be surprised if he was down at Costa's looking for you tonight.'

'Don't be so dramatic,' Christina protested. 'He didn't know I'd be at Costa's.'

But I said I'd probably go to the waterfront cafés, she remembered. She shivered.

Sue said, 'I don't think he's going to give up.' She sounded scared.

Christina could not really blame her. She hoped that the tour left Athens soon.

'I'll go first thing tomorrow.'

CHAPTER THREE

SHE did. And for a week Christina's mind was in two places at once.

One part of her brain was organising hotels and describing antiquities, the other was locked in a timeless embrace with a man she hardly knew—a man who had made sure she hardly knew him. A man who had given her a carefully edited account of himself which had left out all the essentials, possibly including his real name. A man who had said they would never meet again and then, for some unfathomable reason, had changed his mind.

Except that the reason was not unfathomable, however much Christina pretended to herself. It had all been there in the kiss—intensity, anger, *need*. Christina had never felt that she needed anyone before, not in that immediate, physical way. Nor had she felt the same driving need coming back at her, plucking her out of normality and onto a plane where all she could see or touch or taste was him.

'Sex,' she said to herself. 'That's all it is. Strong attraction, sure, but nothing more than a passing thing. Ignore it and it will go away.'

Only it didn't. There were times when she barely noticed her pleasant church group from the American Midwest. They were in Europe for the first time and endearingly enthusiastic about the sights at Mycenae and Delphi. Christina tried hard to share their enthusiasm. She even succeeded sometimes. But the dark, magnetic figure of Luc was always there, always lurking. And all

too often he just swamped the rest. It was not like any
sexual attraction she had ever felt before.

It's not *real*, she told herself.

But it felt real—horribly real. More real than anything else she could remember. It was almost frightening. That stopped her dead in the shadow of a classic
column. He had said that she was afraid of him, hadn't
he?

'Ridiculous,' she said aloud.

But on the long, hot coach journey back to their hotel
Christina was remembering all too vividly every word
he had said. It was nonsense that she was afraid of him.
Of course it was. She was self-possessed and independent and she was not afraid of anyone.

But, if she admitted the truth, there was something in
that dark, demanding presence that sent little chills
through her. Not fear, naturally, but something uneasy
that told her she had no defences against him. Or anyway,
none that seemed to work.

The unwelcome truth was that Luc Henri over-
whelmed her. He had only to look—let alone touch—
and she started to vibrate like a musical instrument played
by a master. And she did not even know who he was!

He might be a villain, she thought grimly, remembering the long dark car that had seemed to be looking
for her. Or merely a businessman, as Geoff had suggested. She just had no idea. She could not even begin
to guess. He had given her no clues at all.

'And that's the problem,' she told the spotty mirror
in her hotel room. 'He told me nothing. Deliberately
told me nothing. He might just as well have been wearing
a long cloak and mask for all I know about him. And
yet he makes me feel like this. I must be going out of
my mind!'

She applied moisturiser to her heated skin and tried
to bring her renowned common sense back into play.

Maybe he didn't own that black limo at all. Maybe he wasn't looking for her. Maybe the meeting at Costa's was pure chance and the limo was crawling along because it had engine problems. Maybe this was all in her imagination. Somehow that was not comforting.

She called Sue from the hotel.

'He's been back to Costa's,' Sue said at once. She did not specify who. She did not need to.

Christina's whole body lurched, as if she were in a lift in free fall.

'What did Costa tell him?' she said, her voice jumping.

'Nothing. You know Costa. A customer is a customer but he doesn't like being pushed around.'

'Oh. What did he tell Costa, then?'

'Not much. He left a telephone number, though. Do you want it?'

She found she did, very much. It was so unlike her. Was she falling in love for the first time in her life?

'No,' said Christina in a kind of horror.

There was a little silence.

'You fancy him,' Sue said slowly. She didn't sound anything like as triumphant as she would have done a week ago. 'It's happened at last.'

Christina did not like the sound of that. Especially in the light of what she had just been thinking herself.

'Nonsense,' she said robustly.

'I saw him kiss you,' Sue reminded her. 'And the way you looked afterwards. Are you seriously telling me he didn't get to you?'

Christina suppressed a little, sensuous shiver at the picture her friend's words conjured up. She repressed it at once.

'A kiss is just a kiss,' she said flippantly.

'So what are you going to do about him?'

The very thought of doing anything about Luc Henri made Christina's head swim. She swallowed, hoping Sue would not detect her confusion.

'I'm not going to do anything about him. I don't know him. What I do know I don't like. He's just too damned sure of himself.' Yes, that was better. Indignation might just get that dark image back to manageable proportions. She added virtuously, 'He's got to learn that he can't go around manhandling people like that in public.'

Sue chuckled unexpectedly. 'What about in private?'

It was a thought that Christina had been trying very hard not to let into her consciousness.

'That is not going to happen,' she said firmly.

She found that her fingers were crossed hard when she put the phone down.

She returned to Athens thoroughly unsettled. There was no sign of Luc Henri. She was not sure if she was relieved or piqued. Either way, it did not help her get the man out of her head.

The next job—crewing for a group of scuba-divers— had been in her schedule for weeks.

'You're getting famous, Christina,' the captain greeted her when she went on board. She had worked for him before and they got on well. He looked amused.

She was startled. 'What?'

'You've set the wires humming,' he told her. 'I must have had three requests for references for you in the last week. What have you been doing?'

She frowned, oddly perturbed.

'I ran out of cash and had to hustle a bit for the next job,' she said slowly.

'Oh, that will be it, then. If the brokers think you're running into problems with money they won't want to put you on a boat stuffed with cash and Rolexes,' he said indifferently. 'Moral: never really *need* a job.'

He gave a hearty laugh and slapped her between the shoulderblades. Christina smiled, but absently.

Was this Luc Henri's master-hand again? Or was she flattering herself? She half wished that she had taken that phone number so she could ring him up and tell him to stop intruding in her life. Except, of course, she acknowledged ruefully, the intrusion might all be in her own imagination. If only she *knew*.

So it was with turbulently mixed feelings that the night they got back to port she went to Costa's for dinner with the rest of the crew. As soon as he saw her, the proprietor finished his conversation and came over.

'Don't tell me,' Christina said with forboding. 'You've been having enquiries about me.'

He looked surprised. 'That's a problem? I thought you wanted a job?'

'Oh, I do,' she said. 'Maybe I'm getting paranoid. What have you got for me, Costa?'

He grinned and flung his arms wide. 'The job of a lifetime,' he said.

Three weeks later Christina toiled up the harbour steps, puffing under the burden of an enormous dustbin bag, and thought hard thoughts about Costa. Job of a lifetime, indeed. Well, she was working for royalty, or supposed to be. That must have been what Costa meant.

All Christina could see was that the yacht was under-provided and seriously ill equipped. Well, she could have lived with that. She had done so before on other jobs. What she couldn't bear was the poisonous atmosphere. It affected everyone, from the ragamuffin crew to the principal passenger's seven-year-old daughter, Pru. Nobody helped anyone and they all threatened to tell tales to the Prince, who had chartered the boat.

The Prince himself, perhaps wisely, had not so far put in an appearance. Instead he had installed his sister and her children and kept promising to join the boat at the next port. He was expected again today in this small Italian harbour but neither the children nor Christina thought he would turn up. The children minded. The

Prince of Kholkhastan joined Costa and the cheapskate Captain Demetrius in Christina's bad books.

Christina heaved the garbage bag onto the top step. 'I'm never going to let it get this heavy again before I dump it,' she promised herself. She straightened, panting, and wiped her forehead before stooping to haul the thing along the dock.

'What the hell do you think you are doing?' rapped out a voice.

Christina stopped dead. She did not believe it. This was fantasy, brought on by heat, exhaustion and sheer temper. Her heart thundered in her ears. She was so startled that if she had not still been holding onto the lumpish bag of rubbish she would probably have fallen back down the stone steps.

She knew that voice. In spite of her best resolutions, she had been sleeping with it for weeks. Cautiously, she looked up.

It was not heatstroke. It was not a hallucination.

'You!'

In some ways, heatstroke or hallucinations would have been easier to deal with.

'What are you doing here?' she gasped.

She stood looking up at him, weeks of studied forgetfulness wiped out by the sheer physical shock of his presence. She had told herself that it had all been an illusion brought on by anger and brief panic when the bank had refused to let her have her money. She had told herself he was no different from anyone else: not a frightening, encompassing presence but an ordinary man, perfectly easy to deal with if you kept your head. And the intensity she had felt beating at her like a flame must have been her imagination. He was probably perfectly indifferent to her.

Luc Henri smiled. His eyes were almost black. He looked tough, powerful and deeply sardonic. Not, thought Christina, recovering herself too late, in the least bit easy to deal with. Or indifferent.

'What are you doing here?' she said again, this time with something like accusation.

Luc reached down. His fingers closed over hers, brooking no resistance.

'At the moment it looks like dustbin duty,' he said drily. It was the suave voice she remembered. This time it hovered on the edge of mockery. It made no difference. That voice had haunted her dreams.

'I can manage,' she muttered, horrified. This was no time to remember dreams that embarrassed her even when she was on her own. Now that she was face to face with the other participant, they were frankly appalling.

Luc seemed unaware of her discomfort. He snorted. 'Don't be ridiculous. That thing is obviously far too heavy for you. What on earth are you thinking of, hauling it around on your own?'

Christina stood very still. A feeling swept over her that made her capable little hands suddenly lose all their usual strength. Shaken, she looked down at his long fingers locked round her own.

No one had made her feel like that, *ever*: as if she was all blood and fire, with no strength or will or ability to do anything but mould herself to him. Mould herself with passion. It was not just the dreams, after all.

'Oh, good grief,' she said, truly horrified.

She surrendered the bag to him, sliding her fingers out from under his without resistance.

He misunderstood the cause of her dismay.

'And it's a great pleasure to see you too,' Luc Henri said, amused.

The heavy bag was no burden to him at all. He swung it up over his shoulder like a sack of coals and turned away. She looked after him, trying to steady herself.

This was no cool, suited sophisticate today. He was wearing jeans and a casual T-shirt which showed

powerful muscles. Christina remembered how she had
sensed that strength under the smart jacket in Athens.
It made something clench in her stomach. She hoped
desperately that Luc was not aware of her turmoil.

Her face burned. The hand which pushed her sunglasses back up her nose shook a little. With his back
turned to her, she flexed her shoulders and the fingers
that he had made feel so frail. Sternly she told herself
to pull herself together.

Luc bore the rubbish off to the prominently placed
bin and returned. He was looking deeply satisfied, as if
something he had planned had fallen out better than he
had expected. It was a very private look. In spite of her
disorientation, it put Christina's hackles up.

'There. Don't try carrying it on your own again,' he
instructed her.

So he was still high-handed. Christina's hackles went
higher. She tried to dredge up the words to tell him
exactly what he could do with his orders. But there was
something in the intent dark eyes which stopped the
words in her throat.

She strove for normality.

'Perhaps you'd better discuss the matter with the man
I work for,' she said in a practical voice.

For no reason that she could think of that seemed to
entertain him. The look of private amusement
intensified.

'Good idea. I might just do that.'

Christina sent a look over her shoulder. She had had
a sharp little argument with the first officer after lunch.
It had culminated in a rude instruction from Captain
Demetrius for her to take the garbage ashore and come
straight back. When she'd set off the captain and the
first officer, who was also his cousin, had been leaning
on the rail, watching her. She was almost certain that
that had been the object of the order in the first place.
Conscious of their eyes on her long, tanned legs, she had

found herself wishing passionately that she had been wearing anything but the standard shipboard garb of shorts and cut-away cotton vest.

Luc followed her eyes. There were no figures at the rail now, but he seemed to read her mind.

'Watching you, were they? No one offered to help?'

Christina shrugged. 'It's my job,' she said levelly. 'Ship's cook gets rid of galley refuse.'

His mouth tightened. 'Not by the tonne.'

'We—er—haven't had the opportunity to unload garbage for a couple of days.'

That was an understatement. Captain Demetrius, seriously out of his depth in charge of a boat all on his own for the first time, had failed to book moorings ahead of their arrival in port. With the early season now well under way, the harbour-masters had turned the *Lady Elaine* away. The captain's new arrogance, presumably acquired by association with his princely employer, had not helped. As a result, so far they had docked in one extremely smelly fishing village, a container port and now this unfashionable harbour.

Luc raised his brows. 'Explain,' he ordered.

Christina sighed. 'Put it this way—it's not the best organised voyage I've ever been on.'

'But—' He broke off whatever he had been going to say, looking suddenly annoyed.

She grinned suddenly, 'In fact it's a disaster. Nothing has been properly planned. The passengers blame the crew. The crew blames the first officer. So they hate him. The first officer hates children. And all but one of our passengers are children. The passenger who isn't a child hates the captain. And the captain hates everybody.'

Luc looked stunned. 'This is outrageous.'

Christina considered. 'Well, no. It's like a board game for adults. Who can you afford to leave alone together on the boat without them killing each other?'

Luc gave an unwilling laugh. 'It sounds poisonous.'

'Quiet,' she corrected him. 'Not a lot of call for conversation.'

Three hours out of Athens the captain had made his first error of navigation. Their passengers were the charterer's sister, the Princess, and her children. All too soon it had emerged that the Princess understood charts better than Demetrius. Indeed, even Christina could read the charts better.

From the moment that had become apparent, the atmosphere on board had become so tense that she could have taken a vow of silence and no one would have noticed.

Her tension must have shown. In spite of her ironic tone, Luc looked at her curiously.

'Will you jump ship?'

'It's a tempting thought. You don't know how tempting,' she said with feeling.

His eyes glinted. 'Then let me take you out of all this.'

That startled her. She jumped and lifted her eyes to scan his face candidly.

'I can't go,' she said in pure reflex.

'Why not? You're wretched. Walk away.'

'It's not as easy as that.'

'It is for a clear-headed girl like you.' He paused, then added softly, 'Unless it's me you don't want to go with. *Do* I frighten you, Christina?'

That was altogether too close to the truth. She lifted her chin.

'I am not afraid of you or anyone.'

'Then let me be your escape route.'

She was thoroughly confused and more than a little indignant. She stared at Luc. He smiled back. The bland expression was complicated, but it was still too full of that private amusement for Christina's liking. She drew herself up a little.

'More and more tempting,' she assured him with her coolest politeness. Then a thought occurred to her that drove the odd tension between them out of her head. She chuckled. 'Especially as I have to tell Simon Aston—one of the children—that he isn't getting the devil's food cake he ordered for tea. But, in spite of everything, I think not.'

Luc did not reply at once. Instead he contemplated her with an odd expression. At last he gave a theatrical sigh. 'Turned down for a schoolboy.'

Christina sniffed. 'A row with a schoolboy. Be precise.'

'Very lowering to the vanity.'

But from the tilt to his mouth Christina was pretty sure that his vanity was undinted. She decided to change the subject. 'What are you doing here, anyway?'

That seemed to disconcert him. Briefly he looked annoyed; then he shrugged. 'Getting away from it all. It's been in the diary to visit this place for a while.'

Which told her precisely nothing. It was quite deliberate, she was sure. Luc Henri was still being evasive. Well, two could play at that game. Christina gave him her sweetest smile.

'I hope you enjoy your holiday,' she said in a tone of unmistakable farewell.

She turned to go. Luc stopped her. He put a hand on her arm swiftly, easily, as if he had every right to take hold of her in that casual fashion. Christina stopped dead, inexplicably shocked, aware that her face was suddenly hot. Her heart pounded.

'I'm serious,' he said. 'I've got a car at the hotel. Come with me now. You need never see these people again.'

Christina shook her head. 'I can't. I signed on for the voyage.'

'Contracts can be broken. Especially if they're treating you badly.'

She sighed. 'It's not the contract.'

A small flame lit in the dark eyes. 'Well, then—'

'I promised,' she said simply.

He stared. For a moment she thought he had not understood what she said.

'I made a promise when I took the job—' she began, but he had understood all right. He was shaking his head in disbelief.

'What does that matter? You don't care about these people.'

It was her turn to look disbelieving. 'I care about my promises.'

He stared. Eventually he said slowly, 'That is very—laudable.'

Her blush was subsiding but she still felt far from at ease. She smiled at him with constraint. Suddenly, startlingly, the brown eyes began to dance.

'So the lady in distress won't let me carry her off,' he said softly. 'What can I do, then? Bring out your dragons.'

Christina could not help herself. She looked at the black rubbish sack and laughed. 'That was about all the tasks I had on hand at the moment.'

He shook his head, seemingly disappointed. 'No dragons at all?'

Christina stared. The way his mouth was tilting, it almost sounded like a challenge.

She thought of Captain Demetrius. Of his cousin, the first officer. Even better, of their absent royal employer who had commanded the whole mess into being.

'None available for slaying,' she said ruefully.

The heavy brows rose. 'You mean there are dragons and you're afraid I won't be able to handle them?' He sounded affronted.

She looked at the broad shoulders and laughed aloud. 'No, no, I'm sure you could handle them beautifully. It's just that if you slay them I'm out of a job. My employer might not feel about promises the same way that I do.'

His eyes narrowed suddenly. 'You're fighting with your employer?'

'My employer is an absentee. It's not easy to fight with a man who isn't there,' Christina said crisply.

His eyes went blank suddenly. 'I don't think I follow,' he said slowly.

'Oh, technically I take my orders from the captain. But the guy who calls the shots is a tennis-playing playboy with an unpronounceable title,' Christina said, selecting freely from what she knew of the Prince. 'He,' she added with some bitterness, 'chose the captain.'

There was a curious little silence.

Then Luc raised his brows enquiringly. 'It really isn't a happy ship, is it?' he drawled.

She laughed shortly. 'I've been on happier.'

The black brows twitched together. He looked at her broodingly. 'This is—irritation,' he said half to himself.

Christina did not understand. It was occurring to her suddenly that he had shown no surprise at encountering her, and that, although he might have had the trip in his diary for ever, she had not the slightest idea who the man really was who owned that diary or what he was doing here.

For a couple of moments during their conversation she had wondered whether he had pursued her to this place deliberately. But his manner did nothing to support that reading of the situation. He found her attractive all right, but whatever he was frowning over at the moment it was not her. If anything, he seemed almost too pre-occupied to remember that she was there.

And yet he was not surprised to see her...

'What are you doing here?' she said again abruptly.

Luc's eyes found hers. He smiled suddenly, brilliantly. 'Reconsidering my strategy,' he said. His voice was full of that infuriating secret amusement again.

To Christina's complete astonishment, he leaned down and slid the sunglasses down her nose so that he could speak straight into her suspicious eyes.

'Don't look so alarmed, Christina Howard. Don't forget, you're not afraid of me.'

He bent his head before she knew what he was about and gave her a light, searing kiss full on her startled mouth.

Then he was gone, slipping like a shadow among the shadows of the waterfront buildings. Christina stared after him. The kiss had been so brief that she was not sure whether she had conjured it up from her fevered imagination.

But then she touched her throbbing lips. It was not her imagination. God knew who he was or what he wanted but, whatever it was, he was *there*.

Irrationally, recklessly, her heart began to sing.

CHAPTER FOUR

CHRISTINA prepared the evening meal on autopilot. Luc was here. Still evasive, still mysterious, but *here*.

She looked in the mirror in her tiny cabin that night and barely recognised herself. Her cornflower-blue eyes were sparkling and her mouth looked softer, fuller, as if inviting a kiss from the unknown. It alarmed her a little but it intrigued her too.

'This is where you find out how much was pure fantasy,' she told herself with satisfaction. It never occurred to her that Luc Henri would not seek her out again. He would not be able to keep away, she knew—any more than she could. She gave a soft, excited laugh.

'Burn, fire, burn,' she told her reflection.

But he did not have to seek her out. She saw him at the little town's smartest hotel the very next day.

She delivered the children to the hotel's sports complex while their mother strolled off in search of more exciting company. Christina lingered briefly. The director of the children's activities was an old acquaintance from previous summers.

'Take care of Simon Aston,' Christina warned Karl. 'He's not as grown-up as he thinks he is.'

'I'll keep an eye out for him,' he promised.

Relieved, Christina made her way up to the lobby. She was dying for a cool drink. That was when she saw Luc Henri. Across the hall, his tall figure was unmistakable. She stopped dead.

He was sitting at a desk in an alcove, below a notice that said 'Press and Office Services'. He did not see her. He was frowning at the screen of a small laptop computer. As she watched he leaned forward and collected a page from the printer, scanning it.

Christina hesitated. For the first time it occurred to her that he could be a journalist. But what sort of journalist? She could imagine him as an international correspondent—one of those soldiers of fortune that patrolled the troubled hot spots of the world looking for their exclusives, even though Athens was hardly hot these days.

Suddenly, she was confronted with another and deeply unwelcome possibility. What if he were a different sort of journalist entirely? This sleepy little port was even less of a hot spot than Athens. What was more, it had no claim to fame either, unless it was the presence of the latest heartthrob, Stuart Define, and his film crew.

Karl had been crisp about them. The actor's entourage had partied into the small hours by the swimming pool, leaving glasses and cocktail detritus to be cleared by the pool attendants at breakneck speed before the first guests arrived to swim in the morning. Now, Christina thought, what if that entourage was about to include a bored and lonely princess? What if Luc Henri were here looking for an entirely different sort of scoop?

As she watched, Luc shrugged. He turned to another machine and fed the paper into it, dialling rapidly. Simon Aston's little face flashed before Christina's inner eye. Her heart twisted.

Well, if that was what he wanted, he would have to think again, she thought suddenly. Luc Henri was not going to get that scoop as long as Christina was on board the *Lady Elaine*. She drew a deep breath, knotted the tails of her shirt more ruthlessly round her tanned midriff and stepped forward.

At once, as if drawn by a powerful, invisible magnet, his eyes lifted, found her. They locked onto her without expression. In spite of that impassive face, Christina sensed a jolt of surprise go through him—not a welcome surprise.

If she had had any doubts about her hypothesis, that reaction would have banished them. He fetched up short, his eyes narrowing. He did not look guilty, exactly, but he did look as if he wished she were anywhere but here in the lobby.

Pretend you haven't seen it, Christina told herself. Pretend you are as naïve as he clearly thinks you are. And get him away before he can see the Princess letting Stuart Define oil her back.

'Hello,' she said with what she hoped was the right touch of girlish enthusiasm.

He detected the false note at once, of course. His brows flew up. 'Hi. Can I flatter myself you're following me, or have you decided to jump ship?'

Christina chuckled. 'Neither, just at the moment. I brought my employer's children for swimming lessons.'

A curious expression crossed his face. 'Your employer was childless the last time I looked.' He paused before adding deliberately, 'And unmarried.'

She stared. 'The Princess is married to an Englishman called Richard Aston.'

'Ah.' His lids dropped but Christina caught a distinct glint in his eyes. 'But your employer,' he said softly, 'is surely the Prince of Kholkhastan? Who, I understand, is still on his travels.' It was not quite a question and there was a distinct edge to it.

Christina made a face. 'Well, if you want to be pedantic...'

'Accurate,' he corrected her. 'I like to be accurate.'

In the reports he filed for his paper? Christina wondered, and felt chilled. He had still not told her who he was and what he was doing here, after all.

She looked at him levelly. 'About everything?'

He looked surprised. 'Of course.'

'Does that include yourself?' she asked sweetly. He stiffened very slightly, but his voice was amused, even indifferent, when he asked, 'Now, what do you mean by that?'

It was the ideal opportunity to confront him with his apparent duplicity. Christina did not know why she hesitated, unless it was because if he admitted what he was she would have to put an end to any future meetings out of loyalty to the Princess. And she did not want to.

She castigated herself furiously but it made no difference. He was high-handed, untrustworthy and much too sure of himself, yet she still wanted to see him again.

But she wasn't going down without a fight. 'Are you saying you've told me the truth about yourself?' she said heatedly.

Luc did not even hesitate. 'I have told you nothing inaccurate,' he said smoothly.

Her blue eyes darted fire and she curbed her feelings with an effort. 'That's not exactly the same thing,' Christina said with restraint.

He looked entertained. 'That depends on your point of view. I didn't think you were the sort of girl who would want a breakdown of my bank balance or my employment prospects.'

Her chin came up indignantly at that. 'Of course I don't.'

He smiled straight into her eyes. It was the dazzling smile again. Christina began to feel a little light-headed.

'Then you know everything you need to make your mind up about me,' he said softly.

She swallowed. It was like being hypnotised. She could not look away. She moistened her dry lips.

'Do I?' It was not much more than a croak.

'Oh, yes.'

Luc did not touch her but from the way he was looking at her it did not make much difference. Christina began to feel that deep, inner trembling that had so alarmed her before. This time it did not feel alarming. If anything it was rather exhilarating.

'Do you want me to prove it?' It was a laughing challenge.

Christina swallowed again. 'I don't know how you could do that,' she said in a tone that tried hard to be sensible.

'That's my problem. Will you give me the chance to try?'

This is crazy, she thought. I ought to tell him that I know his game. I ought to walk away right now. Instead she heard herself say breathlessly, 'Yes.'

The dark eyes blazed. He held out an imperious hand. 'Then come with me now.'

Christina felt as if she was in a dream, as if events would take their course no matter what she did. Slowly she put her hand into his.

He gave a soft laugh. To Christina it sounded triumphant. Even that made no difference, she found. If she had not been in her dream, it would have infuriated her, but all she wanted now was to go with him. He looked down at her, swinging their clasped hands gently.

'Somewhere shady and private, I think,' he murmured.

Involuntarily Christina shivered. Luc's fingers tightened. He made her look at him. For all his insouciance, his eyes were smouldering.

Luc's eyelids dropped. In the middle of her inner turbulence Christina was aware of only one coherent thought: *He feels it too.*

It was alarming. She had never been so sensitive to another human being before, never felt that she could read someone else with absolute clarity—or that he could read her. It was not a comfortable feeling, but that awareness under his down-dropped lids made her feel breathlessly excited. He knew about her turmoil! He shared it!

But at once he was laughing again, the illusion of shared intensity gone. Even as she became aware of the convulsive grip of her fingers on his hand, the mask of amusement was veiling the dark eyes again.

He said softly, 'I wonder if I could displace coffee? Do you know, I almost think I could?'

Christina was bewildered. 'Coffee?'

'Your greatest weakness,' he reminded her.

'Oh!'

She went scarlet, instantly and undisguisably. She could feel his eyes on her, dancing, warm as the Italian sunshine outside the hotel lobby. He looked amused and supremely confident.

But all Christina could feel was sudden cold. This was a practised charmer, she realised with an unwelcome shock. Why hadn't she recognised the signs earlier? If he had confidence it was because it was earned. Women weren't going to say no to a man who could turn their world upside down with a word, a touch. She felt helplessly angry with herself.

Luc didn't notice. He was much too pleased with himself, Christina thought bitterly. He whisked her out through the front entrance of the hotel. He raised a hand to a uniformed man leaning against a car. The other man grinned when he saw them and, in response to a gesture from Luc, threw a set of keys across to him.

Luc caught them one-handed, not letting Christina go for a second. He raised the hand in acknowledgement. Christina watched the way the chauffeur strolled away. So it was not just women who did what Luc instructed, she thought wryly. It did not surprise her.

The keys were to a long, shiny limousine with darkened glass in the windows. It had to be one of the most luxurious cars in the car park. Christina frowned at it. Was it the car that had nosed past the end of the alley outside Costa's? She did not think so but she could not be sure. Would a gossip columnist, no matter how successful, rate a chauffeur-driven Mercedes? It did not seem likely. And yet . . .

'Expense account?' she asked, carefully not allowing her suspicions to show.

Luc was not forthcoming. 'Not exactly.'

He opened the passenger door. Christina stood her ground. 'I don't ride in stolen cars,' she said firmly.

He chuckled. 'Did it look as if I was stealing it from Michael?'

'Michael?'

'The chauffeur. I—er—know him.'

'Oh.' Still she hesitated.

He pinched her chin. 'Don't look like that. He lets me drive the car sometimes, that's all. I've never met such a girl for getting herself worked up over nothing.'

Christina removed his hand from her chin. 'You must know him very well if he lets you borrow a car like this,' she said drily.

Luc was calm. 'I do know him very well.'

Christina was enlightened suddenly. Gossip columnists needed their informants, didn't they? Perhaps the chauffeur was one of Luc's. Another thought struck her. Perhaps Luc thought she was going to be one too.

'Christina, it is hot out here,' he said patiently. 'I want to swim and so do you. Get in.'

Christina felt her dormant annoyance reassert itself at this high-handedness. It was a relief.

'You can't just take advantage of the man like that,' she said with heat. 'What happens to him if you . . . if you keep it too long or—or damage it or something?'

A curious expression invaded his eyes. His lips twitched. But all he said was, 'Do you doubt my driving?'

'That's not the point. Though, some of the roads round here are pretty narrow—it wouldn't be hard to scrape the paintwork.'

'That wouldn't matter,' he said indifferently.

Christina was indignant. 'It might matter to Michael. If he's lent it to you and you damage it, he'll get into trouble.'

He gave her an odd smile, almost tender suddenly. 'He won't get into trouble.'

'You can't be sure of that—' she began, but he stopped her by the simple expedient of putting his hand over her bare wrist. The words clogged in her throat suddenly. She swallowed.

'Christina.'

She did not quite meet his eyes. 'Yes?'

'Let me worry about Michael. Get in.'

She did. He closed the door on her with a quiet thud and went round to the driver's side. He slid behind the wheel, pushed back the driver's seat to accommodate his long legs, and they were off.

Staring straight ahead, she said, 'Before we go anywhere, I want to make it clear that I'm not going to tell you anything about the Princess or her family.'

She looked anywhere but his face. His hands on the wheel were strong and beautifully kept, she noted. She could feel his eyes on her as if he were touching her.

There was a sharp little silence. Then Luc said with an edge to his voice, 'The last thing I want to do is waste our time together talking about Mrs Aston.'

Christina did risk a quick look at him then.

'Another encounter out of space and time?' she asked drily.

His mouth tilted in acknowledgement of the hit. 'I was rather unrealistic there, I admit. No, this time I'll do the thing properly.'

Christina did not ask what he meant. She was not sure she wanted to know. She sat very straight. 'Just as long as you realise I am not going to talk about my employers—'

'They are off the agenda for the rest of the day,' Luc interrupted. She had the impression that he was laughing privately again. 'It will be a relief, to be honest.'

'I don't know what you're talking about,' said Christina, annoyed.

'No, you don't. But you will.'

She bit her lip. When he said 'a relief', did he mean a rest from work? That most of his day was spent following the Princess in the line of duty? Oh, she *wished* he would tell her the truth. She sighed and fell silent.

Luc clearly knew the area better than she did. He took her to a beach further along the coast where you could take a car almost to the edge of the sand. And it was empty.

She opened the car door with an effort that surprised her. 'It's heavy,' she said as he came round to help her.

He shrugged, not answering. Christina got out of the car and caught her breath, forgetting the unusual machine at once.

The scenery was spectacular. The little inlet had been scooped out of a larger bay, so that everywhere you looked there were hills covered with chestnut trees on the higher slopes and silvery olive trees as the ground approached the sea. In front of them, beyond the shimmer of water, a great grey cliff rose up to the sky. But on this side of the bay the slope was gentle and covered in bushes. Bees hummed, the rock-roses bloomed, the air was full of the scent of thyme.

'It's beautiful,' Christina breathed.

Luc was watching her reaction.

'Yes,' he agreed. His mouth quirked. 'Could I have uncovered another weakness?'

She flushed. 'The sea looks so wonderful,' she said self-excusingly.

'Don't apologise. I appreciate a woman who savours her weaknesses as much as you do.'

She knew that she was being teased. But there was nothing she could do about the flush that heated her cheeks, even though it amused him and the last thing she wanted to do was to amuse Luc Henri.

Christina regarded him in considerable dudgeon. She mistrusted him. There was a distinct possibility that underneath that electric attraction she might even dislike him. He had certainly made no attempt to be conciliating. And it was all too obvious that he was used to getting his way without question.

Yet, on the other hand, she reasoned, he was civilised as well as attractive. There was a spark—*something* between them which she had never felt before with anyone else. It made her feel thoroughly unsettled. She was not going to allow herself to get involved too deeply, of course, but...surely she owed it to herself to explore the sensation a little? Purely in the interests of self-knowledge, naturally—so she would recognise it and know how to deal with it if it ever happened again.

Her thoughts broke off there. Christina was too honest to lie to herself. Not allow herself to get too involved, indeed! Look how far she had come already, entirely contrary to normal habits or even her natural wariness of an evasive stranger!

Get real, she told herself. She shook her head ruefully and chuckled. Luc flicked up an interrogative eyebrow.

'Nothing,' she said to him, still laughing at herself. 'Perhaps I need to put a brake on those weaknesses of mine, though.'

Luc grinned. 'That would be a pity.'

She laughed aloud at that, stretching her arms to the cloudless sky. 'I'm inclined to agree with you. Especially in this heavenly place. The sea is probably a magic mirror.' She moved her shoulders in delight. 'Let's swim.'

Luc's eyes were warm with appreciation. He entered into the spirit of her flight of fantasy, pretending amazement.

'In a magic mirror?' he mocked.

Christina sent him a look from under her lashes. 'I bet it makes everyone who swims in it tell the truth,' she taunted pleasurably.

Luc made a face. 'Then I shall have my question ready,' he threatened.

But Christina was too busy twining her hair up on top of her head to be intimidated. She skewered it into place with a couple of pins and untied her shirt to reveal the bikini beneath. Luc watched her with amusement.

'You look as if you haven't swum for weeks.'

'Say days and you'd be close.' Christina kicked off her shoes and thrust her toes into the sand with enthusiasm. 'I got away yesterday but that was the first time since we left Athens.'

He raised his brows. 'You don't swim off the *Lady Elaine*?'

Christina wasn't going to tell him that she didn't like the way the captain's eyes followed her. It made her sound like a wimp. Though that was probably the real reason why she had limited her swimming and she knew it.

'Have you seen the water in the harbour?' she countered instead.

Luc's eyes narrowed. She was not sure he believed the implied excuse, but all he said was, 'You can't spend all your time in harbour.'

Christina gave her bubbling laugh. 'Very nearly,' she said. 'You should see the scrapes the *Lady Elaine* has had.'

'Good grief,' he said blankly.

She wriggled out of her shorts and was ready. She folded her clothes neatly, put them on top of her shoes on a convenient rock and raced into the water. Then she turned back, the water surging gently up to her waist. She flung back her head with delight and saw him standing there with his hands on his hips, surveying her.

'Come on,' she teased. 'Now, this is a weakness that is *really* worth having.'

She scooped the water up in her palms and flung it high, sending up sprays of diamond droplets into the afternoon sun.

Luc stood very still.

Christina shook the brilliant water out of her eyes.

'Come on. What are you waiting for? It's *warm*,' Christina called to him. She flung out her arms above her head, watching the water fountain off them. 'Oh, this is heaven.'

Luc seemed to shake himself. He gave her a sudden smile. It was, she saw, a dazzling one. Irresistible. Oh, well, for once she was not going to fight it. She flashed a smile back at him.

'You could just be right,' he said.

Swiftly he discarded his clothes except for a pair of dark briefs and joined her in the water. Christina had a glimpse of muscular legs and tanned, powerful shoulders, before he plunged into a strong crawl towards the horizon. Laughing, she did a somersault dive in the water and started out after him.

He was too fast for Christina to catch, somewhat to her chagrin. She was a strong swimmer and at the peak of fitness after her job with the diving boat. But Luc was in another class altogether. He could have been an Olympic athlete and in the end she had to admit it.

She stopped at last and trod water, paddling round pleasurably in the buoyant water as she got her breath back.

Eventually he returned. She watched him coming towards her, his long, easy strokes, his body a perfect aerodynamic curve in the water, and a strange shivery feeling started in the pit of her stomach. She had never thought of a man as beautiful before. But, in the sun-filled sea, Luc Henri was beautiful.

What is happening to me? Christina thought, startled and sobered.

He stopped a few yards away from her, shaking the salt water out of his eyes.

'I'd forgotten how good it feels,' he said. 'You were right. Heaven, indeed.'

'Forgotten?' She was surprised in view of that perfect, economical crawl. 'But you're a serious athlete, aren't you?'

He grimaced. 'I was once. These days I don't have the time.' He shook his head. 'Correction. I don't *make* the time.'

Christina was regretful. 'I still wouldn't like to take you on.'

His mouth tilted. 'That's a pity.'

She flushed. 'In a *race*,' she said repressively.

'Of course,' he agreed. His expression was solemn but she knew he was laughing. And then he laughed out loud and it was an infectious, rueful sound. 'Though I don't see why not. You must get more exercise than I do. Want to try? Race you back.'

He gave her a start and, Christina was almost sure, slowed his powerful strokes. She put all her effort into her own but they still arrived neck and neck.

She stood up. 'I concede. You're too good for me.'

She staggered a little under the gentle pull of the tide. He steadied her automatically.

'I wouldn't say that. I thought it was about equal.'

Christina shook her head. 'Only because you wanted it to be,' she said drily.

Luc laughed. 'Then it was.'

She frowned a little. 'I don't like cheating. Winning is no fun if you're handed it on a plate.'

'I didn't say you won, just that we were about evenly matched.'

Christina began to wade out of the water. 'We're not matched at all and you know it. You're way out of my class. There's no point in pretending anything else. I'm not a child. I don't like pretence.'

His brows twitched together.

'You're very austere,' he said, an edge to his voice.

Christina shook her head, making the droplets fly. 'Just accurate,' she said, mimicking his own words back to him.

He looked startled. 'And dangerously acute,' he said, but he said it under his breath.

Christina made her way to the little hollow shaded by rocks where she had left her clothes. She dropped onto the silky sand and stretched her legs out in front of her. Bending forward, she pulled the confining pins out of her hair. The wet mass toppled onto her shoulders. She shook it out.

Luc followed more slowly. He stood looking down at her.

'So you never pretend, Christina?' he asked mockingly. 'No polite evasions? No white lies?'

Christina squinted up at him. She made a decisive negative movement. 'Never. Too complicated.'

His eyes flickered. 'You're right there.'

He dropped down beside her and sat frowning at the empty silver sea. Christina rubbed her hands through her hair. She did not look at him but she was aware of his every small movement, every breath, it seemed.

What is wrong with me? she thought again. She wondered if he could sense it, but a quick sideways look told her that he was wholly preoccupied, a heavy frown between his dark brows.

'So you never lie. It must make you a difficult lover,' he said abruptly.

Christina jumped as if one of the bees buzzing among the olive trees had darted onto the beach and stung her.

'What?' she said blankly.

Luc sent her an unsmiling look. 'How much truth can the average love affair bear?'

She was half-bewildered, half-offended. 'I wouldn't know.'

The dark eyes narrowed. 'No love affairs?'

Christina realised that she had been manœuvred by a master without even noticing what he was doing. She bit her lip and set about recovering the position. Without telling lies, either.

'Enough,' she said carefully. She paused. 'But none of them were average.'

Luc's eyebrows flew up. Christina smiled, well pleased to have disconcerted him. It proved that she had not entirely succumbed to mindless attraction, she thought.

'*Touché,*' he said after a pause. He sent her a measuring look. 'So when do they take place, these far from average love affairs? During the winter? Is that why you're so reticent about what you do between sailing seasons? Do you live with someone?' There was more than an edge to his voice.

Christina was sorely tempted to tell him she did, that there was a man in her life right now. But she had promised herself no lies. She sighed.

'No.'

'So they're in the past?' Luc persisted, oddly urgent.

She shifted her shoulders, annoyed. 'And the future.'

He laughed then—a harsh sound in the warm air. 'That's what you're into? Any adventure, anywhere, any time?'

'Of course not.'

Christina was affronted. She turned her shoulder on him. Luc put out a powerful hand and wrenched her back to face him.

'Why not? A free spirit like you?'

She had not seen him look like that before. His mouth had thinned, his jaw tensed. A muscle worked in his cheek. His eyes were black with some suppressed emotion that looked remarkably like rage.

What have I done to make him look like that? Christina thought, bewildered. But anger swamped her bewilderment as he shook her.

'*Tell* me,' Luc said between his teeth.

'I don't have to tell you a thing,' Christina flashed.

She tried to twitch her shoulder out of his grasp. She met with no success. Instead his fingers tightened almost cruelly.

'Let me go,' she said furiously.

For answer, he pulled her back onto the sand and bent over her. Christina's hands flew to push him away. He caught them in his own and held them down on the sand above her. He bent closer, searching her face. His eyes gleamed.

'All right. Don't tell me. Show me,' Luc said roughly.

She watched as his mouth descended. It seemed to take an age. Her breathing came quick and shallow. Her whole body seemed to vibrate from its core. Her eyes went out of focus and she gave up the fight to keep them open as his lips touched hers, very lightly.

Christina gave a small sob. For a moment the whole world seemed to hesitate in its turning. Then she arched her throat, offering her mouth blindly for his sweet invasion.

It was more than an invasion. It was a whirlwind. When he raised his head she was pliant and trembling. As her eyes opened slowly she saw his face. It looked tormented. Christina was shaken to the core.

'Who *are* you?' he said hoarsely.

She shook her dazed head, trying to collect her thoughts. 'Shouldn't that be my line?'

But Luc was not listening. He was kissing her throat, her heated collar-bone, the vulnerable softness of her inner elbow. He slipped a hand under her to unclip her bikini top. Lost, Christina arched her spine. The soaked material fell away and she felt his tongue-tip trace the sensitive contours of her breast. She moaned.

His hand spread across the small of her back, spanning it as he raised her from the sand to mould her to the length of his body. Released, Christina's arms went round him in a hard embrace. Fiercely she sought his mouth in her turn. One leg twined round his. Luc gave a gasping laugh and they collapsed onto the sand again.

At once he rolled over, taking her with him, so she lay across his hard, warm body. His hand moved with casual possessiveness over her hips. He laughed up into her startled blue eyes.

'Burn, fire,' he said softly.

Christina realised that the possessive hand was getting rid of her last scrap of swimwear. She stiffened. At once he pulled her head down to his, demanding her kiss.

For a moment she surrendered to that blazing magnetism, but at once she was pulling away. She realised that he had grilled her, subtly and effectively, while telling her nothing at all about himself, that what he had told her was almost certainly misleading. Above all, with deep discomfort, she remembered what he had said before they'd set out: 'Somewhere shady and private'!

Had he been planning this seduction even then? Was that why he had not been concerned when she'd refused to discuss the Princess, because he intended to start a summer affair which would give him all the time he needed to get whatever information he wanted out of her? To say nothing of the hold he would have over her if she let that happen.

Christina did not allow men to get a hold over her, ever. Oh, she had plenty of men friends. But she had never wanted serious affairs. Her mother had had too many and they had always ended in tears.

Luc's arms tightened. 'Come back,' he said.

But Christina was already disengaging herself. She rolled away. After an instinctive moment's resistance, Luc did not try to stop her. He lay on the sand, for a moment watching her, and put up a hand to shade his eyes.

The bronzed chest still lifted and fell as if they had been racing each other through the water again. He did not try to disguise his arousal. Christina looked away, conscience-stricken.

'I'm—sorry,' she said with difficulty. 'I shouldn't have—'

He could have been furious. Frustration took people that way. And if she was honest Christina had to admit that he had every reason to believe that she was as aroused as he was, that she would take that arousal to its logical conclusion.

But all he said was a wry, 'You sail in dangerous seas, lady.' Then, more roughly, 'Don't look like that. We both got carried away. *Both* of us. Do you understand? It was entirely mutual. And that doesn't make you a tease for calling a halt, either.'

Christina flushed. She looked round for her bikini top in some confusion. Luc sat up and reached across her. She could not prevent her slight withdrawal from that muscular arm but all he was doing was retrieving the little scrap of material.

'Here,' he said levelly. 'Do you want a hand?'

Christina clutched the bikini top to her and turned her back on him. Silently he stretched it across her sandy back and clipped the fastenings.

'There. Respectable again.'

The trouble was that she did not feel respectable. Not with that small, deep shivering still reverberating through her.

At her shoulder Luc said quietly, 'Stop shaking. Nothing happened.'

Unseen, Christina bit her lip. Nothing happened? Oh, but it had, to her. Obviously not to him, now that the immediate moment of temptation was past. But she felt as if she had been dipped in that magic mirror and come out made of some new material.

Could this be love? Surely not. Not for a man she didn't know. A man she didn't *trust*.

'Oh, Lord,' she said under her breath.

He came lightly to his feet and moved to the water's edge while she scrambled into her shorts and shirt again.

'I'm beginning to see why you're not used to compliments,' he remarked.

Christina was grateful for this return to normal. She looked down at herself and did her best to brush the sand off the cotton garments. She even gave a slightly uncertain laugh.

'That's not kind. I'm not at my best at the moment.'

Luc swung round and looked at her.

'I'm not talking about how you look. I'm talking about how you feel—and what you do about it.'

'I said I was sorry—' she began stiffly.

He interrupted. 'Everyone at arm's length, Christina? Or just me?'

'I told you. I have had my fair share—'

'Of non-average love affairs. Yes, I know that's what you said.' His voice was dry. 'It sounds ideal, admirably under control. Has it occurred to you that one day you just might find you're not in control any more?'

'No,' said Christina sharply, although it was exactly the suspicion that was beginning to grow and grow inside her newly made body. It scared her half to death.

She looked at him. Even in swimming trunks, with his drying hair wildly untidy, even speaking in that quiet, reasonable voice, Luc Henri radiated an arrogance which was all the more powerful for being unconscious. She had never met anyone like him before. It was breathtaking.

Christina realised suddenly that that arrogance must have grown out of his making other people do exactly what he wanted for years and years. She straightened her shoulders. Well, not me, she promised herself. Never me!

She ran her fingers through her hair and said with assumed lightness, 'I need to be getting back. At least, if I'm going to keep my job...'

Luc looked at her. His eyes were black. He seemed to be hanging onto his temper by a thread.

'And that's all?'

Christina shrugged and picked up her shoes.

'I know it's the nastiest job I've had for a long time but it's all I've got. At least there's only another three weeks to go.'

Luc glanced at the sea. 'A lot can happen in three weeks.'

'I know,' she said with feeling. 'On present form, I just hope it doesn't include drowning.'

He seemed to hesitate. 'Or meeting your employer, presumably,' he said at last.

Christina was surprised. She had forgotten the detestable, absent Prince. She made a face. 'He may not turn up. Even if he does, I don't expect the cook will have much to do with the great man. As long as he pays my wages—I don't have to be in love with him.'

There was an odd, charged silence. Then Luc said slowly, 'No, you don't, do you?'

CHAPTER FIVE

LUC'S mood seemed to change after that. He still smiled but he seemed to have gone away somehow. Christina was chilled. She could not think what she had said to make him retreat like that.

Unless, she thought suddenly, talking about the Prince of Kholkhastan reminded Luc that he had a job to do and that he was hardly getting on with it. She decided it would be a good thing to make it plain how little she knew about her employer before he decided to try to pump her for information.

'Where is Kholkhastan?' she asked, in pursuance of this policy.

He frowned. 'Don't you know?'

'I'd never heard of it until I took this job.'

He shrugged. 'You're not alone. It's a small principality in the Himalayas.'

'A principality? Isn't that rather unusual?'

'Say unique and you'd be nearer the mark.' Luc sounded remote, almost bored, yet Christina detected some sort of feeling there—a feeling he was deliberately hiding from her, she was sure.

'So how did it come to be?'

He shrugged again. 'Who knows? A combination of chance, superpower diplomacy and sheer bloody-mindedness probably.'

'I don't understand.'

He looked out to sea, his eyes narrowing. 'In the nineteenth century, the British Empire came face to face with the Russian Empire in the Himalayas. When both sides had lost enough battles, they decided to leave the re-

79

maining nations intact as a buffer between them. During the twentieth century, the others got taken over or had revolts. Kholkhastan survived. It was too small and too remote for anyone to bother to invade.'

'No internal revolts either?' asked Christina, fascinated.

'The ruling family were very conscientious. The good of the people came before personal gratification. So there was nothing much to revolt against.'

'That doesn't sound like the tennis-playing playboy I've been hearing about,' Christina said drily.

An odd expression crossed his face. 'You don't want to believe everything you hear,' he said harshly. 'He pays his dues.'

She stared, her suspicions reviving. 'Are you sure you don't know him?'

He seemed to shake himself. 'You could get that out of any newspaper library. If you were interested.'

Christina shook her head vigorously. 'I'm not. I just want this job to be over. Then I'm away. Too many tensions.'

The moment she said it she could have kicked herself. Not that Luc said anything, but from the way his eyes narrowed Christina suddenly found herself remembering that he could well be a journalist. The last thing the Princess and her children needed was for Christina to chat to the world's press about the fiasco that was the *Lady Elaine's* current voyage.

Before he could demand further details, she said hurriedly, 'It must be getting late. I should go back.'

She scrambled to her feet. Luc looked irritated but did not try to dissuade her. He drove her back to the *Lady Elaine* in barbed silence.

When they arrived he brought the limousine to a halt at the end of the quay. He turned off the engine and turned to her.

'Thank you,' said Christina swiftly before he could speak. She heaved down on the doorhandle. It was remarkably stiff.

'Christina—'

'It was a lovely swim,' she interrupted, still pushing at the handle. 'I— What is wrong with this door?'

'Central locking by the driver,' he said with complete sang-froid. His eyes laughed at her. All hint of his earlier remoteness had gone. 'When am I going to see you again?'

'What?' Christina stopped attacking the doorhandle and stared at him. 'Are you telling me you've locked me in?'

Luc looked amused.

'Entirely for your own safety,' he said soothingly. 'You might have fallen out at any of those hairpin bends. When?'

Christina pushed back her hair with hands that trembled a little. 'I don't go out with men who turn locks on me,' she flashed.

He flicked a switch on the driver's console. There was a soft click. 'There, you're free. When?'

He looked into her eyes. The amusement was superficial. Underneath it, she could see, he was tough and very determined. Quite suddenly Christina stopped trembling. She was shaken by that expression—and the intensity with which she wanted to see him again, in spite of everything. 'Dangerous seas', she reminded herself, her mouth drying.

He had not given her a convincing explanation of his presence in the little port. She was almost certain that he was here snooping on the Prince's family for some gossip column. Two good reasons not to see him again. And the wild way her heart was beating made a convincing third.

This was no time to hedge, she realised suddenly. No vague implication that she would see him when she had

some free time would do. This was important. She had
to state her position and hold to it. Stand your ground,
she told herself.

She took a deep breath and said quietly, 'I don't think
that's a good idea.'

She thought he would contradict her but he was too
clever for that. Instead his mouth tilted cynically. 'You
are almost certainly right. When?'

Christina shook her head. 'You don't understand. I
mean—'

'I know what you mean,' Luc said harshly. 'I even
agree with you. We know nothing about each other but
it's obvious we don't have much in common. There are
more reasons than I can count why it would be better if
we didn't meet again.'

Christina was bewildered. 'Then...'

Luc reached out and took her by the wrist. The words
died in her throat.

She sat there looking at him dumbly. Her pulses thundered. His thumb moved over the softness of her inner
wrist in a caress as light as thistledown. He must be able
to feel her blood racing under his fingertips, she thought
muzzily.

'Some things have nothing to do with reason,' he said.
He sounded almost angry.

Close to, the dark eyes had flecks of amber in them.
They were quite unreadable. Christina watched, mes-
merised, as the handsome head descended.

She thought confusedly, Grown men, sophisticated
men don't go kissing girls in cars as if they were
schoolboys on a first date. *I* don't kiss people in cars.
I'm not some sex-starved adolescent. I don't *believe* this.

It was not like the other times. On the beach Luc had
been quite simply bent on seduction. In Costa's he had
been angry—angry with her and, if Christina was any
judge, angry with himself. He was not angry any more.
Not angry but not—quite—in control either.

He kissed her with long, slow sensuality. Practised sensuality. Christina just managed to recognise it, though her senses were whirling and her hands clung to him in spite of herself. His lips were soft, barely making contact, but her skin felt as if it had been sensitised through to her bones by his touch. She quivered as his lips travelled from her mouth to the vulnerable hollow at the base of her throat. She felt the tip of his tongue there, very gentle, utterly devastating. Her eyes closed and her head fell back with a soft moan.

He gathered her up against his body. She went to him bonelessly, mindlessly.

He murmured something, sounding shaken. His words were blurred against her skin but it did not sound like any language that Christina had ever heard before. In her present state that hardly surprised her. Nothing about this encounter bore any resemblance to anything that had ever happened to her before.

She moved in his arms, arching towards him. He caught his breath. For a moment he went very still, as if she had surprised him. Christina opened dazzled eyes.

He was looking at her mouth. His eyes had gone almost black. There was a blind, hungry look about him. In other circumstances that look would have alarmed Christina. Here, now, it charged her heart with a sort of fierce triumph.

His eyes lifted, met hers. Oh, yes, the passion was unmistakable. Christina was shaken by the depth of that passion. And it was not anger. But it was not wholly welcome to him either, she saw. Beneath the passion there was a cynicism, a bleakness even. As she watched, his mouth tilted wryly. It looked as if he was acknowledging some private joke—a joke against the whole situation.

Christina stared, chilled, even as her body still resonated to his touch. Was he laughing at her or himself? And which would be worse?

'Reason?' he murmured. 'I think I forgot what it was the moment I saw you.'

He was suddenly closer, his face so near that it made her dizzy to keep him in focus. Her suspicions seemed suddenly irrelevant. Christina closed her eyes.

Luc's hands were in her hair, holding her head to receive his kiss. It was not the kiss of a man who was laughing at her.

Christina forgot that Luc was a stranger, that he had told her nothing about himself, that he had followed her and ordered her about in a way that she did not accept from anyone. She forgot that he was probably spying on the Princess.

In fact she forgot, as if it had never been, her whole careful policy on avoiding involvement, which had carried her unscathed through six Mediterranean summers. She forgot principles, prudence and even common sense. All she knew was that something deep in her recognised Luc's kiss—and rose up to meet it.

For a few wild seconds, her desire answered his. His hands moved on her body in unquestionable mastery. Scarcely aware of what she was doing, Christina lifted herself towards him. Luc's kiss grew suddenly fierce. She did not protest. She gloried in it. Arms clutched across his warm shoulders, she was as demanding as he. When his hand moved from her hip to her thigh and beyond, all the wariness which had protected her on the beach deserted her. She had no thought of denying him.

Then he said something strangled and almost flung himself away from her. He was breathing hard. There was no private irony in his expression now, just a wild blaze of feeling. Unmistakable feeling, thought Christina, shaken. She recognized it because she shared it. As, presumably, he could see.

She put an unsteady hand to her mouth. It was swollen.

The flame in his eyes was dying down. He searched her face. He looked astonished.

'I'd forgotten,' he said softly, half to himself.

Christina felt a tiny flicker of anger. He had kissed her into a daze of delight and he was talking to *himself*?

'I hadn't,' she said with a return of acidity. 'It's Costa's all over again.' She remembered what she had felt then and whipped up her anger. 'You really think you can do any damn thing you want, don't you? No matter where. No matter to whom.'

Amusement lit his eyes. Luc took her hand away from her mouth and surveyed the tremulous softness of her lips.

'I? I wouldn't say I did that unaided,' he remarked.

Christina tugged at his hold. It made not the slightest difference. He barely seemed to notice.

'Let me go.'

His eyes were steeply lidded. They made him look cool, in control—almost bored by being in control. It added fuel to her anger.

'I said, let me go.'

He smiled lazily. 'As soon as you tell me when I'm going to see you again.'

'You're not,' she said instantly.

It was pure instinct. She needed to defy that lazy control. She hauled at his grip on her wrist again. Without effect.

'That's plain unrealistic,' he said with odious patience. Would nothing puncture that assurance?

'No,' Christina almost shouted.

He gave a silent laugh. She twisted violently in his grip, her wrist dragging painfully. She bit back an exclamation. The only notice he took of her efforts was to carry her hand to his lips. Looking into her blue eyes all the time, he brushed his mouth across her knuckles in the lightest of kisses.

Christina recognised a challenge when she saw one. She abandoned the attempt to retrieve her hand and tried to take a grip on herself. She did not like the appreciative amusement in his eyes at all. It had to be quenched.

'I said no,' she told him more calmly but with great firmness.

There was a little silence. Half-nervous, half-furious, Christina tossed her hair back. 'I said—'

She stopped as Luc's eyes flared. Then the sleepy lids drooped. 'Don't do that,' he said softly.

For a moment she was bewildered. She shook her head in confusion. 'Do what?'

'That,' he murmured.

At last he let go of her hand. Christina gave a gasp of relief. It turned into something very different as he reached out. He slid his hand under the flying softness of her hair.

Christina's breath stopped as if he had stabbed her. She was shaken by the sensation of his long fingers, warm and secret, against her neck under the cloak of her hair. She moistened suddenly dry lips and swallowed. She saw him watch the little reaction and wished suddenly, passionately that she did not suspect what he was and what he was doing here.

His gaze on her mouth, he said, 'Or that.'

Christina felt her face flame. Suddenly she could not bear it any more. She said abruptly, 'Who are you, Luc Henri?'

His lids veiled his eyes at once. He went very still. His hand fell from her neck. The man of secrets was back with a vengeance, she thought. When he looked at her at last, Christina detected wariness.

'It's taken you a long time to ask that,' he said slowly.

This time she was not quick enough to suppress the wince. 'So you admit it needs to be asked?'

His mouth twisted but he looked her coolly in the eye. 'I admit nothing.'

'Not even that you haven't been straight with me?' she flashed.

His eyes flickered. 'It depends what you mean by straight.'

'Don't play games with me—' Christina burst out. She could hear the naked pain in her voice and stopped at once. But it was too late.

She was hurt and she was not skilful enough to disguise it. The pain was easy for anyone to detect, if he had any intelligence at all. And whatever else she suspected about Luc Henri she had no doubts about his intelligence.

That cry shifted the balance of power between them radically. It forced her to admit, in spite of herself, that Luc was more than a stranger, no matter how strongly she resisted it. And that made her suddenly too involved. An unwelcome thought, brutal in its clarity, surfaced out of the warring instincts: if she was involved, she was also vulnerable.

Luc Henri recognised it too, she saw at once. He was not chivalrous enough to pretend that he did not.

'Well,' he said on a long, marvelling breath.

Christina writhed inwardly. His satisfaction was blatant. She would have given everything she owned to recall that involuntary cry.

But it was too late.

Trying to retrieve her position, she said desperately, 'I don't care who you are or what you're doing. I just don't want to be dragged into anything.'

Luc was watching her as if she fascinated him. 'Don't you?' he murmured at last.

Christina stared, not understanding.

'Care?' he elucidated.

'Oh!'

Both hands went to her cheeks in pure distress.

'Don't hide from me,' said that quiet voice.

She shook her head, horribly embarrassed.

Luc pulled her hands gently away from her hot face. 'No, don't. There's nothing to be ashamed of. Surely you know that, a liberated lady like you?'

The mockery was not unkind but Christina flinched from it.

He went on evenly, 'Spend the night with me.'

She froze.

'Neither of us is an innocent. We both know where we're headed.' He sounded impatient. 'Why drag it out? Don't go back to the damned boat. Forget the captain. I can give you a better time than that.'

Christina found her voice. 'I'm sure you can.' It did not sound like her voice at all. She cleared her throat. 'I mean could.'

His eyes were very dark. 'No, you mean can.'

She shook her head. She compressed her lips to stop them trembling. For one brief, crazy moment she thought of going away with him—away from the Princess and whoever she might choose to socialise with. Away from the boat, somewhere distant and private where Luc could take her in his arms and . . . She stopped herself with an effort that was almost physical.

'No.' It was all she could manage. It scraped her throat like sandpaper.

He looked incredulous. 'Are you going to say you're not that sort of girl?'

That hurt too, but Christina learned fast. She had seen it coming and hid the instinctive flinching more successfully this time. She raised her head and met his eyes squarely.

'I don't have to make excuses, Luc,' she told him quietly. 'You asked me to spend the night. I said no. End of story.'

He frowned. 'Why not?'

This was awful. She could not say, Because I want to so much that you could convince me black was white.

She kept her voice steady with a supreme effort. 'I don't have to give you reasons either.'

He was unmoved. 'You do when you kiss me like that.'

The eyes that met hers held a challenge, and this time there was no amusement whatsoever. Christina lifted her chin.

'All right. Tell me, then. Is Luc Henri your real name?'

He hesitated.

Christina pressed on. 'And aren't you as much interested in the Princess Marie Anne as you are in me?'

Luc looked wary and amused in equal measure. 'I wouldn't say as *much*,' he drawled.

Christina refused to back down. 'But if she weren't here you wouldn't be here. Would you?' she flung at him.

He shrugged, looking bored. 'Maybe.'

'Don't lie to me, Luc. You're following her, aren't you?'

His eyes narrowed. 'What do you mean?'

Christina took one look at his bleak expression and decided that her sympathies lay with the Princess. 'You weren't in that hotel by chance. I saw you at the fax machine.'

'Really?' He was clearly not going to explain himself. He sounded icy.

Christina refused to be intimidated. 'Really,' she said with spirit. 'What's more I wouldn't spend the night with you if you were...were...'

'The last man on earth?' he prompted, his eyes glittering.

She glared. 'I was going to say, the Emperor of China, but it amounts to the same thing.'

He stared at her as if she had struck him. There was a sharp silence. A muscle worked in his temple. Christina put her hand on the doorhandle. His mouth hardened.

'Doesn't it just?' he said at last.

'Goodbye.'

She turned away, opening the door.

'You'll walk away from—?'

He stopped as she swung back on him, suddenly savage. 'From what, Luc? A few kisses? A man who was quite willing to hound me through the backstreets of Athens in a damn great Mafia limo? A man who can't even tell me anything about himself because he doesn't want me to know what he does for a living?' Her voice spiralled upwards.

Luc stared at her. She had the impression that he was utterly taken aback. It was some balm for her wounded feelings, but not much.

She drew a shaky breath and said more quietly, 'I don't know what sort of girl you think I am, Luc. But I can tell you what I'm not. I'm not the sort of girl who spends the night with a man she can't even *trust*.'

She flung herself out of the car without waiting for his reply. She ran along the quay and scrambled quickly down the slippery steps where the car could not follow. She leaned back against the warm stone wall, her blood pounding in her ears.

She did not know how long she stood there, the sun on her closed eyelids. Her breath slowly came back to normal. Luc did not follow her.

Eventually she heard the expensive engine start and purr away down the sweep of the harbour road. When she looked, he had gone.

Christina sank shakily down onto the sun-warmed steps. Her brain was whirling. Not just her brain, either. Physically she felt as if she had just withstood a tornado, every nerve alert, every muscle trembling faintly. And when she touched it her mouth was tender.

How can a man affect me like this? she thought. Especially one I don't know and don't trust!

She could find no explanation. Oh, there were plenty of excuses: he had startled her, she had not been braced to resist him, she had never met anyone like him before, she was trying to protect the children and the Princess by removing him from the hotel in the first place...

But Christina was honest enough to admit that they were only excuses. She had gone with him, stayed with him for hours because she was deeply attracted to him, maybe was even a little in love with him. In spite of the heat haze she shivered. It was not a pleasant thought.

She had never felt like this before about anyone. She had never had to face this tension between attraction and deep mistrust. She did not know what she ought to do. She did not even know, in her heart of hearts, what she wanted to do. She only knew that she did not want to think about the invitation she had rejected in case she regretted it too bitterly.

That was where Christina stopped her thoughts dead in their tracks. 'Who are you kidding?' she muttered aloud, despising herself. 'You don't want to think about it in case you change your mind!'

The thought was so alarming that she banished the whole subject. She stood up with resolution. There was still a job to be done. And first the children had to be collected.

When she got to the hotel she did not even think about going through the main reception area. That was where she had encountered Luc Henri last time. This time she made her way round through the garden to the sports complex. In the distance, a couple were hand in hand. Christina took in their quiet air of perfect harmony and winced.

Luc had teased her, ordered her around and kissed her nearly senseless. He had not held her hand. She wished he had.

Sharply she turned away. It was nonsense, of course. Luc had not been thinking about love or anything like it. He had offered her a night of passion and, if she remembered correctly, a good time. Pacing in a sunlit garden, hands and eyes locked in mutual absorption, had not been on his agenda at all.

And don't you forget it, Christina adjured herself. But she still ran down the path to the sports complex as if all the demons of jealousy were after her.

The children were waiting, perched on bar stools that were too high for Pru, sipping importantly at violent-coloured drinks. The barman grinned at Christina's look of horror as she came up to them, panting.

'Dinosaur's Blood,' he said, nodding at Pru's sundae glass of fizzing purple mud. The ice-cubes in it were green. 'Speciality of the house. Mainly cherry cola.'

'Oh,' said Christina, slightly reassured.

Pru negotiated the bendy straw into the corner of her mouth and said pleasurably through it, 'We've got a secret.'

Simon kicked her. 'No, we haven't.'

Pru rocked. However, she remained upright. It showed the experience of a girl who had had bar stools kicked from under her many times, Christina thought wryly.

Pru clung to her point tenaciously. 'You said we could tell Christina.'

Simon frowned. He stared out at the garden with heavy meaning. Pru continued to look at him mulishly but Christina followed his eyes. And stiffened. The anonymous lovers had wandered into view, still hand in hand. They were no longer alone, though. This time they were surrounded by a laughing group of tanned and beautiful people whose manner said that they knew everyone in the place was looking at them and that it was no more than they expected. Among them was the Princess.

Christina looked quickly at Simon. For the first time since she'd joined the *Lady Elaine*, the Princess was not looking bored or bad-tempered. She was laughing at something one of the women had said to her. It made her look mischievous and incredibly beautiful. It was clear that that was what the movie star thought too.

Watching the famously handsome Stuart Define watch Simon Aston's mother, Christina felt her heart sink. Poor child, he knew his mother was bored and lonely and he was quite old enough to add two and two and make five. Quite as capable as any underhand gossip columnist anyway, she thought. All her protective instincts rose. She hated Luc Henri at that moment.

But all she said, very gently, was, 'If it's your secret and you want to tell me, that's fine. But I don't think you should tell me anyone else's secrets. You might be wrong, you know.'

Simon looked hugely relieved. Christina's heart twisted. She ruffled his hair suddenly. He looked surprised and scrambled off his seat.

'Come on,' he said in his usual lordly way. But Christina thought he was quite pleased, even though it was beneath his dignity to admit it.

They went back to the boat. The first officer met them at the gangway with a spate of complaints: Christina should have come straight back, she should never have stayed ashore so long; there had been someone from the port authorities on board screaming at them about some trivial infringement of their petty bureaucracies; she should have been there to interpret; the captain was very annoyed.

Since all this was delivered in Greek in an angry undertone, the children were not supposed to understand it. But Simon was acute.

'They've got you into a mess again,' he deduced.

Christina sent him a harassed look. 'No, they—' She met his eyes and remembered that it was no use trying to lie to children. 'Oh, hell,' she said, giving up. 'What if they have? It's not kind to gloat.'

Simon looked surprised. 'Uncle Kay will have to come and sort it out,' he said simply.

It was clear that he looked forward to that eventuality with a lot more enthusiasm than Christina did. She nearly said so, but his love and trust in his uncle was too evident, so she bit her lip.

When he summoned her to his presence, Captain Demetrius shouted at her enjoyably for ten minutes, then dismissed her with instructions to make sure she gave the crew a decent dinner for once.

'Yes, sir,' murmured Christina, straight-faced.

Much pleased by this exercise of his authority, he waved her away. In the galley she gave way to mirth.

'Oh, well, my heart may be broken,' she told the spotty mirror over the sink cheerfully, 'but at least I can still laugh in the wrong places.' Then she stopped, shocked by her own words.

Heartbroken? After four meetings, three kisses and one indecent proposition? Ridiculous.

She was still telling herself how ridiculous it was, when the intercom beeped.

'Christina, would you come to the main stateroom, please?' said the Princess.

Relieved to go back to what she was paid to do, Christina went. She half expected to find Stuart Define and his friends there, but they were not. Instead the Princess was sitting in the padded seat under the porthole, one arm round Pru, to whom she had been reading. Simon was sprawled on a Kashmiri rug, reading a book of his own.

'I want to give a dinner party on board,' she began.

Christina nodded. The film people, she surmised. She fished her notepad out of her pocket. 'How many?'

The Princess grimaced. 'Depends. Eight or so, I suppose. We can't expect my husband to be here, of course.' There was an edge to her voice.

Simon did not look up but he began to kick the rug ferociously. Christina said nothing but her heart went out to him.

His mother did not seem to notice. 'Nor my brother, from the looks of it. Really, it's too bad of them.'

Pru looked up from her position in the crook of her mother's arm. 'Uncle Kay is coming,' she announced.

Simon turned his head.

The Princess gave her a squeeze. 'Yes, darling, of course he is. We just aren't sure when.'

She met Christina's eyes over the top of Pru's head. 'Men,' she said. 'I don't care for myself but I can't bear it when they let the children down.'

Christina did not comment. She hardly needed to. She and the Princess were at one on the subject. The absent Prince could not have slipped much further in her estimation anyway, so she was not surprised by this revelation.

In fact, she thought wryly, there was only one man who came lower on her personal scale of values and that was Luc Henri. Which made it all the more crazy that a bit of her was still regretting that she had turned him down.

There was the sound of running feet on the deck above them. Violent voices followed. Christina recognised one or two key words. She put down her notes.

'I think,' she said carefully, 'I've just realised what the port authorities wanted. Excuse me, madam.'

She pelted out of the stateroom and up to the bridge. Alarmed, the Princess followed.

The captain was nowhere to be seen. Two of the crew were standing there looking worried. A small boat was racing across the water towards them. The harbourmaster was standing in its stern with a loud hailer. Fierce Italian fell about their ears. Christina winced.

'We were supposed to move,' she said to the crew crisply. 'They want to berth that big yacht over there here. We should have cast off ten minutes ago,' she added, in an edited translation of the screams from the launch.

She became aware that the screams were being answered in equally excitable Greek. Instead of moving the *Lady Elaine*, the captain and his first officer were leaning over the side, enthusiastically exchanging bilingual insults.

One of the sailors in the launch saw her and said something to his master. Captain Demetrius followed the pointing finger. He swung round, looking up. He saw her.

'Get down here,' he yelled, adding an unaffectionate epithet. 'Tell that idiot I don't understand a word he's saying.'

It was only Christina's professional standards that made her obey him—that and the faint, dwindling hope that she might be able to avert disaster. It was hopeless, of course. Translating, hauling on ropes that had got too wet to handle properly, running to pass information between Captain Demetrius and the harbour-master in the launch, Christina could see it coming.

Watched by excited children and a disbelieving Princess, the captain took the *Lady Elaine* through a series of complicated manoeuvres that seemed to take for ever but did not move her appreciably from her original mooring. Meanwhile, the big yacht, coming beautifully in under sail, got close and closer.

The harbour-master danced with fury and frustration in his launch. 'Have these morons ever taken a rubber duck into the bath with them?' he roared at Christina. 'Do they know anything about steering?'

She did not translate that.

And then the captain gave one last, exaggerated turn to the wheel. Slowly, gracefully, the *Lady Elaine* swung her bow out to sea and rammed full into the side of the yacht.

The Princess screamed. The captain swore. The harbour-master flung his loud hailer into the air and howled. The children looked on with sparkling eyes.

And Christina sat down on the bottom step of the companion-way, dropped her head in her hands and gave

IT'S FUN! IT'S FREE!

HOW TO PLAY

BIG BUCKS

It's so easy... grab a coin, and go right to your BIG BUCKS game card. Scratch off silver squares in a STRAIGHT LINE (across, down, or diagonal) until 5 pound signs are revealed. BINGO!... Doing this makes you eligible for a chance to win £600,000 in lifetime income (£20,000 each year for 30 years) Also scratch all 4 corners to reveal the pound signs. This entitles you to a chance to win the £30,000 Extra Bonus Prize! Void if more than 9 squares scratched off.

Your EXCLUSIVE PRIZE NUMBER is in the upper right corner of your game card. Return your game card and we'll activate your unique Prize Draw Number, so it's important that your name and address section is completed correctly. This will permit us to identify you and match you with any cash prize rightfully yours!

FREE BOOKS PLUS FREE GIFT!

At the same time you play your BIG BUCKS game card for BIG CASH PRIZES... scratch the Lucky Charm to receive FOUR FREE Mills & Boon Enchanted™ novels, and a FREE GIFT, TOO! They're totally and absolutely free with no obligation to buy anything!

These books have a cover price of £2.10* each. But THEY ARE TOTALLY FREE; even the postage and packing will be at our expense! The Reader Service is not like some book clubs. You don't have to make any minimum number of purchases - not even one!

The fact is, thousands of readers look forward to receiving six of the best new romance novels, at least a month before they're available in the shops. They like the convenience of home delivery, and there is no extra charge for postage and packing.

Of course you may play BIG BUCKS for cash prizes alone by not scratching off your LUCKY CHARM, but why not get everything that we are offering and that you are entitled to? You'll be glad you did!

THE READER SERVICE: HERE'S HOW IT WORKS

Accepting free books places you under no obligation to buy anything. You may keep the books and gift and return the invoice marked "cancel". If we don't hear from you, about a month later we will send you 6 additional books and invoice you for just £2.10* each. That's the complete price, there is no extra charge for postage and packing. You may cancel at any time, otherwise every month we'll send you 6 more books, which you may either purchase or return - the choice is yours.

* Prices and terms subject to change without notice.

way to helpless laughter, until she became aware of
Simon standing in front of her, his eyes gleaming.

'Now,' he said with immense satisfaction, 'Uncle Kay
will *have* to come and take charge.'

CHAPTER SIX

CHRISTINA stood up. 'Oh, I think we can manage without His Highness,' she said, ruffled.

She smoothed her hair, curbed her giggles and went to assist negotiations.

'Where do you want us?' she asked the harbour-master, at last.

She was editing Captain Demetrius's inflammatory speech with abandon. It was clear that the harbour-master knew it. He glared at the captain.

'Where I want this floating traffic hazard is somebody else's harbour,' he spat, but he could not resist corn-flower-blue eyes. He sighed. 'You are persuasive, *signorina*. And I suppose I would not want it on my conscience that I let Captain Blood up there loose on the high seas again. Very well. But you tell the Prince that he gets a new captain or this boat does not leave port. Understood?'

She nodded diplomatically but under her breath she said, 'Gee, thanks.'

When the launch had gone, zipping over the waves like an angry wasp, she eyed Simon thoughtfully. She had been entertaining a suspicion about Simon for several hours. From the complacent look on his face now, she was almost certain that she was right.

'Simon, you know how to get in touch with your uncle, don't you?'

Complacency dissolved into consternation so fast that it was ludicrous. 'I don't know what you mean,' he hedged. 'Mother calls his office . . .'

98

Christina pursed her lips. 'I'm not talking about your mother. I'm talking about you. I think you could speak to him right now if you wanted to. In fact, I think your uncle Kay may be a lot closer than anyone thinks. And you know it even if your mother doesn't.'

Simon went red.

'Uncle Kay says Mummy is a nuisance,' Pru remarked chattily. 'Do you think he'll say the captain's a nuisance as well?'

'I should think he'll say we're all a nuisance,' said Christina, her antagonism fanned by the small girl's artless confidence. What right had the man to be saying such things to Pru about her mother? Especially as he could not even be bothered to join the cruise that he had sent them all off on. 'Simon—'

'Oh, no. He likes you,' Pru said with confidence.

But Christina was narrowing her eyes with intent at Simon. She flapped an irritated hand at this diversion. 'Your uncle Kay doesn't even know I exist.'

'Uncle Kay knows *everyone*,' Pru said proudly. 'Sir Goraev says that's what makes him a great man.'

'Who is Sir Goraev?' snapped Christina. 'Court flatterer?'

That went over Pru's head. It was probably just as well, thought Christina. This situation was hardly the children's fault.

Pru was struggling to explain Sir Goraev. 'He runs things. He ran things for my grandfather too. He's very old and doesn't like people. But he likes Uncle Kay.' She was obviously quoting. 'Uncle Kay never forgets any of his depin-dipen—'

'Dependants,' Simon supplied. His colour had returned to normal. He gave Christina a bland smile which set her teeth on edge.

'I, however, am not one of his dependants,' Christina snapped, quite forgetting that this was only a child. She caught herself, irritated, and sighed. 'Simon, you're a superior little beast. I hope you're eaten by a giant jellyfish.'

He grinned, unconcerned.

But Pru was still on the old tack. She shook her head obstinately. 'Uncle Kay knows all about you. He said—'

'Pru!' Simon stopped grinning.

Pru made a face but did not say any more. Christina wondered what their absent uncle had said to them. Something to worry them, from the looks of it. She reminded herself firmly that it was none of her business.

She went back to the kitchen and made a pastry case for a beef Wellington. She found herself bashing the pastry as if it were a personal enemy. As if it were the Prince of Kholkhastan, she thought with grim self-mockery.

As a result of the day's disasters, the evening meal was late. Everyone succumbed to temper, from the children, who were overtired, to the captain. Demetrius whiled away the interval before dinner by drinking his way steadily through a bottle of brandy and received his tray from Christina with a slow smile that made her grateful that she had put on a long cotton skirt against the night air.

'This is horrible,' said the Princess, pacing the top deck restlessly after a screaming Pru had finally been coaxed into bed. 'It's supposed to be a holiday and I spend my time refereeing tantrums. Not all of them children's.'

Christina nodded sympathetically. She tidied coffee-cups from the family meal onto a tray.

'I'd really like to go ashore.' The Princess looked wistfully at the harbour. 'It's not that late. I could meet a couple of friends. Maybe dance. Would you—er—cover for me?'

While she met Stuart Define?

'I'll keep an eye on the children,' Christina said carefully.

'Well, Pru anyway. Simon probably won't let you. He's holed up playing computer games in his uncle's study.' She sighed. 'I don't know what's got into my son, Christina. He's been so *rude* lately.'

Christina concentrated on the exact placement of a silver sugar bowl on her tray. She did not look at the Princess.

'Perhaps he's missing his father,' she suggested in an even voice.

The Princess's conscience did not seem to be touched. She snorted. 'He should have got used to that by now,' she said harshly. 'My husband is like my brother. They compartmentalise. Women and children come in a very small compartment.'

Christina was startled into looking at her. The beautifully made-up face looked tight, as if the Princess was trying not to cry.

She said, 'Have you got a boyfriend, Christina?'

'We-ell—'

'The boy the children were talking about—the one who teaches them swimming?'

'No,' said Christina.

But the Princess was too absorbed in her own train of thought to hear her. 'Well, let me give you some advice: don't let any man get a hold on you. Men are like children—the moment they see you're fond of them they reckon they can do anything they like and you'll put up with it.'

Christina's thoughts flew at once to Luc. She had accused him of thinking that he could do any damned thing he wanted. It seemed he was not alone. He had been pretty sure of her. 'Why drag it out? Don't go back... I can give you a better time.' Oh, yes, he fitted the Princess's pattern all right. Had he detected that she was fond of him, then? At the thought her whole body burned.

'I believe you,' she said with feeling.

'You're a nice girl, Christina,' the Princess said unexpectedly. 'Don't let them do it to you.' She looked at her watch again. 'Hell, I'm going. What have I got to lose? See if you can get Simon to bed by midnight. I'll see you in the morning.'

She went. Christina washed up, set various trays for breakfast and went out onto the foredeck.

Most of the crew were ashore. The captain and his cousin were working their way down a second bottle of brandy and did not emerge from the bridge. The only light was in the study where Simon was presumably still playing with his laptop computer. Or perhaps he was watching a video.

Christina groaned inwardly. It was probably something violently unsuitable. No doubt it was her responsibility to stop him. She went to investigate.

But Simon was not watching any of the expensive screens with which the study was provided. Simon was using his mother's mobile telephone. He had his back to the door. He sounded angry and upset.

'I know, I know. But we can't *wait*.' He paused and then said clearly in answer to some question, 'What? Nobody.' Another pause, then, 'When? Oh, that's great. See you then. She *will* be surprised.'

He clicked off the phone, pushed down its aerial and folded the mouthpiece before putting it down on the desk. Christina closed the door quietly. Simon jumped and swung round.

'Oh—Christina.' He sounded more than startled. He sounded slightly guilty, she thought. 'I didn't hear you. I thought you'd gone with Mummy.'

Christina eyed him narrowly. 'Was that what you were telling your father?'

Simon looked puzzled. 'My father?'

'Isn't that who you were on the phone to?'

Enlightenment dawned. 'Oh. No. That was my uncle.'

Having her suspicions confirmed so comprehensively was surprisingly unrewarding. In spite of her sympathy for Simon, Christina's mouth tightened. 'Do you report in daily?'

Simon flushed. 'Uncle Kay told me I wasn't to tell,' he began unhappily.

She softened at once. 'It's all right. It's not your fault. Your uncle told you to call him and you're only doing what you think is right.'

And if I ever get my hands on that uncle I shall tell him what I think of men who expect children to spy on adults, she promised herself silently.

Simon did not look comforted. 'He's coming now,' he blurted out.

'Is he?' Christina said gently. 'That's all right, then, isn't it?'

'I wasn't supposed to tell you,' Simon muttered.

She put an arm round his shoulders. 'It's all right. I won't tell anyone else. Anyway, when will he be here? Tomorrow? Or the day after? So we won't have to keep it secret for long.'

Simon bit his lip. 'Er—no.' He squirmed out of her hold. 'I think I'll go to bed. I'm very sleepy.' He gave an exaggerated yawn. 'Goodnight, Christina.'

'Goodnight,' she said, puzzled.

He went. She tidied up, closed the door after him and went slowly on deck.

It was a beautiful night. The stars were vivid. If you half closed your eyes you could imagine them rushing towards you on an icy, burning wind. Christina shivered, rubbing her arms. Like the icy burning at the core of her body when Luc Henri touched her, she thought wryly. Memorable but all in the imagination. Oh, why couldn't she get the man out of her head?

She paced the boat restlessly, trying to do just that. She was not very successful. There was no one else about and her thoughts kept straying back to him, no matter how much she tried.

Remember he lied to you, she told herself. Remember that. You found the strength to turn him down. You can't weaken now. Why let him back into your head the moment you're on your own again? Pull yourself together, for heaven's sake, or you'll be a sitting duck if he comes back...

She swallowed at the very thought. He wouldn't come back, she assured herself. Surely he wouldn't. She had turned him down in no uncertain terms. And he had not *said* he would be back. Besides, he still had his beastly job to do. If he continued his pursuit of her, he had no guarantee that she would not shop him to the Princess.

Yet... She shivered. She had dismissed him comprehensively when she walked out on him in that Athens café. And it had not noticeably deterred him. He had found her in Costa's. He had been quite prepared to stalk her along the Athens waterfront. Who was to say that he would not do it again? If he did, was she strong enough to remember he had lied to her, used her, or tried to? Was she strong enough to go on saying no?

In the warm dark Christina swallowed. She was not at all sure.

She leaned on the rail and looked towards the little town. Was he still there? Was he prowling the hotel, waiting to capture the Princess and Stuart Define in some beautiful, disastrous photograph? And if so, was he thinking of her? Or had he dismissed her from his mind while he got back to the serious business of pursuing his career and his life?

Almost certainly the latter, Christina thought. She moved restlessly. She hated the thought that he could forget her. Especially as she was having no success in doing the same with him.

'Vanity,' she told herself. 'That's all it is—offended vanity that he got to you more than you got to him. Not very nice but not deadly either. *Forget* him.'

She was still trying to convince herself that it was a matter of will-power when the gangway creaked. Startled, she peered down into the darkness. It could not be one of the crew. They made a lot more noise than that after a few hours ashore. Could it be the Princess back so early?

She leaned over the side, straining her ears. This time it was easier to hear—a firm tread on the creaking boards. No, definitely not the Princess. A thief? Her heart lurched at the thought. Could someone have been watching the *Lady Elaine*? Seeing the Princess and most of the crew leave, had someone deduced that the boat was deserted and come on board to see what he could pick up? If so, it would have to be dealt with.

Christina ran on silent feet to the deck below. The man, whoever he was, did not seem to be worried about detection. He was not even trying to disguise his presence. He was a tall figure in the shadows, wearing some sort of pale shirt and dark trousers. She had the impression of height and a lean, competent strength as he vaulted over the railing and onto the deck.

He stood there for a moment, looking around. He was taking his bearings, she saw. Her indignation rose as she watched him survey the place as if he had every right to be there. Christina's fear was swamped with sheer outrage. She stepped forward out of the shadow of the overhanging deck.

'Looking for something?' she flung at the dark figure.

He froze momentarily. Then, slowly, he turned.

'You.' Her voice was odd in the darkness. It took Christina a moment to recognise the feeling: naked shock. And then she had a blaze of irritation. 'I should have known.'

The shock was not all she recognised, and it was mutual. The intruder was Luc Henri, and it was clear that he was so far from coming in search of her that he was downright furious to have encountered her like this.

She took a step backwards. 'What are you doing here?' It was an accusation.

Luc ignored it. 'What are you—?' he countered. 'Simon said— That is, I thought everyone had gone ashore.'

'So I guessed,' Christina snapped. 'What are you looking for? Love letters? Incriminating photographs? Or were you thinking of grilling the children?' She was almost weeping. With fury, she assured herself.

He stared at her in the darkness. 'What are you talking about?'

'You deliberately waited until the Princess had gone ashore, didn't you?'

'Waited?' Luc shook his head slowly.

'You're playing games again,' Christina said wearily. 'I know you've been following her. I saw you coming out of the hotel's press office.'

He shook his head again. 'I don't see the connection.' He sounded puzzled.

She said suddenly, harshly, 'How much are they paying you? Or is this a freelance assignment and you sell to the highest bidder?'

'Sell...?' Luc sounded completely blank.

She took a hasty step forward. 'I could *hit* you,' she said in choked voice. 'Why won't you tell me the truth?'

He stared down at her in the darkness. A slight breeze was stirring her soft hair out of the hastily tied ribbon at the back of her neck. He seemed not to be listening to her. He reached out and stroked a couple of the escaped fronds. The sensation of his fingers barely touching the vulnerable softness below her ear stopped Christina from breathing for a moment. She gave a gulp.

His hand stilled at once.

'This is a hell of a time,' he muttered.

Then he pulled her to him, so suddenly that it jerked her off balance. It was almost rough. It was also as if he could not stop himself. In the cool dark, his mouth was hot and searching.

Christina responded like a parched forest catching fire. She was helpless to do anything else. In his hands she lost all power of rational thought. She knew it and despised herself for it. It made no difference. She held him as fiercely as he held her and gave him kiss for kiss.

When he let her go they were both breathing hard.

'A *hell* of a time,' Luc said again. His voice was not entirely steady, but that note of private laughter was back. He pushed a hand through his hair and looked down at her, not letting her go. 'So what are we going to do about it, Christina, my lovely?'

She was shaken. 'I'm not your lovely,' she said, trying to regain her sanity. 'I—'

He gave her a soft laugh. 'Still not happy with compliments? But you are, you know,' he murmured. 'You only have to look in the mirror.'

'To see I'm lovely?' She put all the amused disdain that she could manage into her voice. 'I've been looking in the mirror for nearly twenty-four years without clocking that one.'

Luc flicked her bottom lip with a casual finger. It spoke of total possession more eloquently than words. The words she was about to add died on Christina's tongue.

'And to see you're mine. Maybe the one depends on the other,' he said provocatively.

'*No,*' she said in a strangled voice.

But he had taken her into his arms again. He dealt swiftly with the top she was wearing. One hand went to her breast, teasing, tantalising. The other sustained her as she swayed. Christina heard herself moan. It appalled her but there was nothing she could do about it.

'No?' Luc taunted softly.

His touch was a delight and a torment. Christina's head fell back.

'Please—don't do this to me,' she said raggedly, all pride gone.

He bent over her. In the dark his eyes glittered. In a strangely rough voice he said, 'What do I do to you that you don't do to me?'

His hands moved to her hips, pulling her hard against him. He moved explicitly. Christina felt her senses whirl. She clung to him as the stars dipped and swayed behind his shoulder. The deck lurched under her. She was shaking.

Luc ran his tongue along her exposed collar-bone. Her skin quivered at the twin assaults of the night air and his warm mouth. He felt her reaction instantly. He laughed.

'You're mine, aren't you?'

It felt like a taunt. Christina could not deny it but she would not give him the satisfaction of admitting it out loud either. She shook her head silently.

It annoyed Luc. In the darkness she felt rather than saw the movement as his heavy brows twitched together. He shook her a little.

'Tell me you're mine,' he ground out.

His hands slid lower, pressing, caressing. It was a torment to deny him, but she had to if she was going to hold onto any self-respect at all.

'I—can't,' said Christina on a gasp.

They both knew that she was saying no to a lot more than the spoken command. His hold tightened.

'*No,*' she said on an agonised breath. 'No. Listen to me, Luc. Be sensible. You shouldn't be here.'

'I know exactly where I should be. Where we should both be.' There was a laugh in his voice. He nuzzled her throat.

Christina tried to lever herself away from him. Without success.

'I'm not joking,' she said, though her senses were flaming and her voice was far from as resolute as she would have liked.

That seemed to amuse him even more. 'Neither am I.' His face moved against her skin. 'Mmm, you smell like heaven. What is it?'

'Salad dressing,' snapped Christina, trying to prise herself out of his arms.

He gave a choke of laughter. 'The sexiest salad dressing in the world.'

'I wish you'd stop laughing at everything I say.'

'And *I* wish you'd stop talking.'

Luc's mouth closed over hers in precise illustration of his meaning. Christina gave up trying to extract herself from the powerful embrace and tried instead to use the unavoidable interval to collect her thoughts. It was not easy.

He lifted his head.

'You're not concentrating,' he said reproachfully.

Christina was grim. 'Oh, yes, I am.'

'No, you're not. I have a great deal of experience in this area and I can categorically state—' He broke off abruptly, his head lifting.

Christina froze too. She held her breath, ears strained.

'What is it?' she whispered at last.

'I'm not sure.'

'Did you hear someone?'

Luc sounded abstracted. 'Maybe.'

He put her away from him and turned to face the upper deck, still listening. Christina took the opportunity to readjust her top. It had sunk to her waist but somehow she found the straps and hauled them up over her shoulders. She was not at all sure that she had the thing on the right way round but it would have to do. She seized his arm.

'The captain's supposed to be on watch. He could have come down for another bottle,' she said urgently under her breath.

'Possibly.'

Luc was still alert, still scanning the decks. He seemed to be paying no attention whatsoever to her. Christina was too anxious to be resentful, however.

'You'd better get out. He's got a nasty temper, especially after a day like today.'

He sent her a quick, unsmiling look. 'What happened today?' he said sharply.

Christina winced. 'Look, Luc, can you forget you're a reporter just for a few minutes? Just long enough to get off this boat? Please?'

He went very still. 'A reporter?'

'I told you, I saw you,' she said impatiently. 'That's not important. What is important is that they don't find you here. I don't imagine the Prince would be very keen on journalists snooping round his boat. It's probably trespass or something. And he doesn't sound like the sort of man who would forgive and forget.'

He was staring at her in the darkness. 'A *reporter*?'

There was a definite flurry of footsteps on the planks over their heads. Christina was in an agony. She shook his arm impatiently, indicating the gangway with its pretty awning bleached grey in the moonlight.

'Go *on*.'

Luc must have heard the footsteps too. He ignored them.

'But if I'm a reporter shouldn't you be hanging onto me, giving me up to the proper authorities?'

She was pushing at him now. He was immovable. It was maddening.

'Well, yes, in theory, I suppose. But—'

'So why don't you?' he asked softly.

'And why don't you stop interrogating me and just take your chance before I change my mind?' Christina urged, exasperated.

'Yes, why don't I?' He sounded really curious.

His hand slid round her waist, whipped her close to him. His fingers slid under the thin fabric of her top, making a mockery of its careful readjustment.

'For heaven's sake, go,' Christina urged.

'Call out and have me thrown off,' he invited.

'Don't be ridiculous.'

'Now, why is that ridiculous?'

'Because . . .' But she was not sure of the reason. She just knew it was.

'After all, you don't trust me. You've told me that at least three times today.' His voice was suddenly hard. 'You kiss me like a woman in love but you won't spend the night with me. You keep telling me to go away. So why not just call for help and get the whole thing over with?'

A woman in love? Oh, Lord, no, prayed Christina silently.

She arched as far out of his hold as she could get. 'I don't want to stir up trouble for the sake of it,' she muttered, distracted.

Even to her own ears it sounded feeble. Luc looked down at her scornfully. 'Why not, if you seriously want to get rid of me?'

'I—'

But she couldn't answer him. There wasn't an answer. He had found out what she had been hiding even from herself. She did not seriously want to get rid of him. She did not trust his motives, she did not believe a word he said, she knew that he was clever and resourceful and probably ruthless, but when he held her in his arms she took a step into another dimension.

She forgot the Princess to whom she owed loyalty, or the children to whom her heart had gone out. Most of all she forgot what she owed to herself: a decent self-respect, protection for her vulnerabilities, defiance of her dignity. All she remembered was Luc.

'Oh, God,' Christina said on a sob.

'My darling—' His voice was suddenly urgent, but there was a new flurry of footsteps, this time ones which could not be ignored. They pounded down the companion-way, light and fast and no longer furtive. The beam of a powerful torch came on abruptly, raking them from head to toe.

Luc put her quickly behind him, but not soon enough to prevent the light dazzling her. Christina flung up a hand to shield her fractured sight.

Luc rapped out, 'Turn that thing off.'

To her astonishment he was obeyed at once. She fell back against the railing, her eyes screwed tight and watering.

So it was with particular clarity that she heard Simon's young voice say, 'Uncle Kay?' and then with huge relief and pleasure, 'Uncle *Kay*.'

CHAPTER SEVEN

CHRISTINA'S eyes flew open. As they adjusted to the dark, she saw Simon Aston clinging to Luc Henri's tall body as if he had known him all his life. A horrid suspicion began to dawn that he was not a journalist after all. She shrank back against the railing until it bruised her spine. She barely noticed.

Uncle Kay?

Luc had put his arms round the boy instinctively. As she watched, he touched Simon's head. It looked like a gesture he had made many times before. Uncle Kay! Christina turned cold as she took in the implications.

'You didn't say when you were coming,' said the boy in muffled accents.

Luc said calmly, 'It's all right. I'm here now.'

It sounded as if he had said that many times before, too. If there had been any doubt who he was, that automatic tone of comforting reassurance would have dispelled it. But there wasn't. None at all.

Christina struggled to assimilate it. Luc Henri was not a reporter. He had followed the Princess here all right but not to reveal her indiscretions in the international press, and certainly not to woo an itinerant ship's cook. She would only have ever been incidental to the Prince of Kholkhastan—an amusement or an annoyance, depending on how co-operative she was, but essentially unimportant. And for a while she had even suspected that he was following her!

The night was suddenly very cold. She clasped her arms round herself and felt goose-flesh under her fingers.

113

God knew why he had decided to travel incognito. No doubt he had his reasons for it—probably international security. Making a fool of her had been purely a side-benefit, Christina thought in gathering wrath.

But it was not just wrath. It was pain as well—pain and a horrible, wincing humiliation. Try as she would, she could not get out of her head his mocking words of just a few minutes ago: 'You kiss me like a woman in love.'

It couldn't be true. Now more than ever it *must* not be true. She had thought that he could turn her world upside down. She had thought that he could make her say black was white. She had thought that he had the power to hurt her. She had not dreamed by how much—or how foolish and alone she would feel.

I wouldn't spent the night with you if you were the Emperor of China, she had said. Well, to all intents and purposes he might just as well have been. Thank God I didn't, thought Christina fervently. How much worse would the humiliation have been if I had? How much worse the loneliness?

Luc was talking to Simon in a low voice. Christina might not have been there, for all the notice he was taking of her. It was chilling in one way. In another, she was thankful. She did not know what she could say—to either of them. She had never felt so completely at a loss in her life.

Fortunately Simon did not seem to have noticed her behind his uncle. Or perhaps he had forgotten that his torch had illuminated them deep in a passionate embrace. Christina shivered involuntarily, remembering that passion. It had vanished now as if it had never been. Clever, lying Luc was not going to waste his time when there were important family matters to be dealt with, she realised. Cold clutched at her heart.

'Mummy hasn't come back,' Simon said in a high, agitated voice. Then he seemed to recollect himself and detached himself from his uncle's embrace a little self-consciously. 'Daddy rang and I went to look.'

Luc ruffled the boy's hair. Christina saw it with an odd little clutch of the heart. It somehow made him even more remote from her.

'Well, if he rings again you can tell him I'm here.' Luc paused. 'Anyway, you were hardly on your own with Miss Howard on board, were you?'

The clutch of the heart was suddenly savage. So that was what she was to Luc now. Miss Howard! Except, of course, that he was not Luc Henri. He was the autocratic and unfeeling Prince of Kholkhastan. And he had lied to her from the beginning to the end of their acquaintance. He had made an almighty fool of her. He had teased her, pursued her, all but seduced her—and all of it without a glimmer of compunction.

Hell, thought Christina, righteous anger beginning to assert itself at last, he had even been prepared to take her to bed with him without telling her who he was. How deep could treachery go?

Treachery goes with indifference, a small, cold voice said in her ear. If he *cared* he wouldn't have treated you like that. If he cared even the least little bit, he would have told you who he was. He would have trusted you, no matter who else he had to hide his identity from.

Unseen, Christina shook her head. She was bemused by how much it hurt. She had known that he was lying to her, after all. Or at least that he was not telling her the whole truth. But the depth of those lies!

She could have flung herself on the deck and wept. Fortunately the anger kept her upright and dry-eyed.

Simon shuffled his feet. 'I didn't know Christina was still here,' he muttered.

'And that was why you called me?' asked his uncle. 'Were you scared on the boat on your own?' He sounded sceptical.

Simon hesitated for a moment. Then he shook his head. 'I wanted you to bring Mummy back,' he blurted out.

Luc sighed. 'Simon, you're too old for this. I told you last time—'

'She *listens* to you,' his nephew interrupted.

'Then she's the only one on this boat who does,' Luc said wryly. He turned his head and said over his shoulder, 'Come here, Miss Howard. My nephew appears to have cried wolf for no reason.' His voice was bleakly and absolutely indifferent.

Even as she winced, Christina understood that he wanted to defuse the intensity of the situation for the boy. All right, she could not wipe out what had just happened, but she could pretend that she was as indifferent as Luc was. If she was careful, she might even still salvage her dignity. She stepped forward.

'I didn't realise you were worried, Simon,' she said, constraint and remorse at war in her voice.

She did not look at Luc. She felt him stir restively beside her but he did not attempt to touch her—not so much as her hand.

No doubt the Prince of Kholkhastan had a well-tried set of rules when it came to conducting his illicit affairs. They would not include holding hands with the lady of his choice in front of the children. Or, presumably, in front of anyone likely to realise who he was and what he was doing, Christina realised, raging inwardly.

That must have been why he'd taken her off to that deserted cove. She had thought that he wanted to be alone with her, whereas all he'd wanted was to be out of sight of people who would recognise him. Her whole body burned with indignation.

Simon said in a small voice, 'I'm sorry, Christina.'

Christina did not know what he was apologising for, but his uncle clearly did.

'We'll say no more about it,' Luc said sternly before she could answer. 'But it's got to stop, Simon. Do you hear me? I can't jump every time your mother goes out for the evening. And you're old enough to know it.' He sounded weary all of a sudden. 'Now go to bed. It's late.'

The boy did not move. 'Will you be here in the morning?'

Christina thought that Luc sent her a quick look but in the shadows cast by the moonlight she could not be sure.

'I'll be here,' he said. 'Go to bed.'

But still Simon was not satisfied. 'And the secret . . .?'

'The secret is out now,' Luc said grimly. 'Go on.'

Reassured at last, Simon turned and ran up the companion-way. Halfway up he remembered his manners. He paused, looking down at them in the darkness.

'Goodnight, Christina. Goodnight, Uncle Kay.'

'Goodnight,' said Christina, wondering if this were a delaying tactic to postpone bedtime. If so she had no objection to assisting him. She had not the slightest idea what she was going to say to his uncle when Simon left them alone.

His uncle, however, had no such reservations. Before she could say anything he had stepped forward, looking up at his nephew with determination. 'Bed,' he said firmly.

Simon laughed. And went.

The silence he left behind him was loaded.

'Damn,' Luc Henri said softly.

No, not Luc. The Prince of Kholkhastan. Christina moved away from him.

'If you'll excuse me, I will say goodnight as well,' she said. She paused before adding with bite, 'Your Highness.'

He seized her by the shoulder and brought her sharply round to face him.

'Don't play games,' he said roughly.

Christina was rigid with anger—anger and hurt—but she decided not to look at the hurt for the moment. Her head went back. She glared up at him in the darkness.

'*Games?* How dare you accuse me of playing games? I've never told you a lie,' she mimicked savagely. 'I dare say you didn't. You're very good at deception, aren't you? Did you tape the evidence to *prove* that everything you told me was strictly accurate? Accurate and as untrue as hell because you never told me the important thing.'

'Is my title so important?' he said coldly.

'Who you are is important,' she flung at him. 'You know it is, or you wouldn't have bothered to hide it. And you have the gall to tell me not to play games!'

His angry breath was audible. 'It wasn't a game,' he said, very soft.

He kissed her. It was savage.

For a moment Christina was nearly lost. Even in his anger, he was who he was and she responded to him, heart and mind and body.

Then she remembered that he was not a prying and secretive journalist; he was worse. He was a powerful man who had played with her as if she'd been a puppet from the first time he'd borne her off for coffee. Shame flung itself over her like a suffocating blanket. She choked and pushed him away.

'How dare you? Is this the way you usually treat your employees?'

He drew back. 'All right. I should have told you. I admit I was wrong. I'm sorry. OK?' He sounded goaded and not in the least apologetic.

Christina gave a scornful laugh.

'You don't understand. A man in my position has to be careful.'

The humiliation was like a scorching flame. It choked her. 'I'm sure you're fighting off predatory females all the time,' she agreed, when she could speak.

'Not—'

'Only, if you remember, I wasn't the one doing the pursuing. You were the one in the damned great car, tracking me through the backstreets of Athens. In fact, you were the one who chased me to that café in the first place.' A thought occurred to her. 'I didn't have a chance of getting away, did I? You could do anything you wanted, couldn't you? A man in your position.' She mimicked his tone bitterly. 'You were the one who was making enquiries about me all round Athens. You got me this job, didn't you?'

His fingers tightened till they bit to the bone, but when he spoke it was with his arrogant drawl, as lazy as it was indifferent.

'Of course.'

'God, I hate you,' Christina said, meaning it. She could feel his eyes on her in the dark, as if he could pierce the shadows by sheer force of will alone.

'Aren't you overreacting a little, darling?'

'I am not,' said Christina with cold fury, 'over-reacting. And if you call me "darling" again I will push you over the side.'

His eyes gleamed. 'Try it,' he invited. His voice was full of amusement—and a sort of lazy promise that she recognised even in her anger.

Her heart leaped. She stepped back. 'I'm going to bed. With or without your permission.'

'Running away?'

'Only from the irresistible urge to kick you,' Christina assured him. 'I don't relish being lied to.'

'Then let me explain,' he said reasonably.

She feared that reasonable voice. It could persuade her of anything. She backed away. 'No explanation could cover it—not lies on this scale.'

'Very dramatic!' he said drily. 'Christina, don't be an idiot.'

'I wasn't, until you made a fool of me,' she said with bitterness. 'Did you enjoy it? You really are very clever at lies. No, sorry, not lies—evasions. I suppose you've had a lot of practice.'

'No, I haven't, as it happens,' he said furiously. 'I've never been in such a damnable situation in my life.'

Christina's lip curled. 'Poor Luc.' She paused. 'Or should I call you Your Highness all the time? I wouldn't like to presume.'

'If you call me Your Highness again, I won't be answerable for the consequences.'

Christina found that she believed him. She refused to let it intimidate her.

'So is Luc your real name?' she flung at him.

He hesitated.

'See,' she taunted. 'Titles are safer, aren't they?'

He took a furious step towards her. She backed again. It brought her up against the bulkhead with nowhere else to go. Luc kept coming. He curved over her to lean against the wall, one arm on either side of her shoulders, effectively trapping her.

'I have a number of names,' he said evenly. 'Luc is one. Henri is another. So is Alexander. After assorted grandfathers, ancestors and well-wishers. One day I'll be happy to give you the full roll-call. *Now* I just want you to listen to me for two minutes.'

Christina decided that in the circumstances it would be prudent to do so. She lifted her chin, though.

'I'm listening.' Her tone was not conciliatory.

Luc sighed. 'You're not making this easy.'

'Good.'

He said suddenly, harshly, 'It was necessary. I was responsible for my family's security. A man like me is always a target. That makes anyone close to me vulnerable as well. I had to be sure you were who you said you were before I could let you join the *Lady Elaine*.'

Christina's chin did not come down a millimetre. 'So you asked everyone I'd ever worked for?'

'Not quite. There were gaps.'

None of the captains she had worked for had ever been interested in what she did in the winter months, so they could not have told his snoops. Christina was fiercely glad that she had managed to keep something of herself private from his probing. Even though it was by accident.

She said mockingly, 'I'm surprised you dared to take me on, in that case.'

'Much against my private office's advice.'

'Am I supposed to be flattered?'

'Don't be facetious.' His voice was clipped.

'I'm not. I take this very, very seriously.' The mockery fell away. Her tone became pure steel. 'I've never worked for a man who spied on me before.'

'I . . . was . . . not . . . spying.'

'Oh, I think you were. Spying and testing me out. To see how much you could get me to tell you about myself.'

'You don't know what you're talking about.'

'I assure you I do. I was there, don't forget. Tell me, as a matter of interest, was seducing me part of the strategy of the investigation, or just a chance bonus?'

He laughed—not a pleasant laugh. 'If you think I seduced you, then your experience is even less than I thought.'

Christina could have screamed. She had walked right into that one. She set her teeth. 'Well, what were you trying to do? Prove that you could get a girl into bed who didn't know you were a prince? Ego needs a bit of a boost does it, *Your Highness*?'

There was a sharp little silence. She could not make out his expression in the shadows, but Christina had the impression that he was outraged. Presumably he was not used to people speaking to him like that, she thought savagely. Well, if he had told her who he was in the first place, she would have behaved properly. Now he would get what he deserved. When he lied and cheated, he forfeited all rights to courtesy from her.

She told him so, the words tumbling over themselves.

Luc stiffened. 'You really think you've got it all worked out, don't you? Has it not occurred to you that I could have been trying to protect you?'

Christina laughed.

He was coldly impatient. 'This is ridiculous! You don't have the slightest idea what my life is like. Until you took this job you'd never even heard of me, had you?'

'Should I have done?' Christina said as nastily as she could. 'I admit I don't read the gossip columns.'

'I'm not talking about gossip.' Luc pounded his fist against the wooden bulkhead behind her. He sounded as if he was about to explode. 'I'm talking about dissidents, international terrorists: men with guns and bombs who think taking out someone like me would be good public relations.'

'*Wh-what?*' Christina was shocked.

'I'm a target,' he said. He sounded tired suddenly. 'I have been for years, ever since I became a UN negotiator. When I meet a girl I—like, I have to be sure that she is what she seems. That she's not a plant. That's she's not dangerous—to me or to the people around me. When I'm going to spend time with the children—well, it becomes doubly important.'

Christina had got her breath back. 'I understand that,' she said without expression.

'Then—'

'And I understand something else as well. In spite of my limited experience—' she mimicked his voice again '—I understand that you saw me and decided you would have me—no pretty nonsense about meeting a girl you like, if you please. This was a straightforward acquisition from the start. You bought me with this job the way you'd buy the stores and the bottled gas.'

He said nothing. In the dark she could feel his eyes on her like lasers. She could feel the anger in him. Oh, no, the Prince of Kholkhastan was certainly not used to being spoken to like this, thought Christina. She ignored it. She felt triumphant at ignoring it.

'You tracked me down. You put a "sold" sticker on me. And you waited for the results of your investigation. Efficient. Not very human, perhaps, but efficient. I'm impressed.'

'No, you're not. You're in a rage.' He sounded amused again all of a sudden. 'But I can—'

She swept on. 'And then you got your report on me. You must have done because you wouldn't have let me come on the boat with the children otherwise. So the report must have said that I was no international terrorist. What a relief. You didn't need to worry any more about what I might do if I knew you were the Prince of Never-Never Land.'

'Kholkhastan,' he interjected quietly. She did not think he was laughing any more.

Christina waved aside the interruption. 'So what does our concerned, responsible hero do then? Does he come down and talk to this girl he says he likes, like any normal human being? Tell her who he is? Tell her why he behaved like that? *No!*'

'Christina . . .' It sounded like a warning.

But she was not about to be warned off. She took a hasty step towards him in the dark. 'No. What he does is carry on pretending. Now, why could that be?' she mocked. 'Would you like to hear my theory?'

He made a strange, wild gesture, abruptly stilled.

'I'm sure you're going to tell me,' he said quietly.

She bared her teeth. She was in such a temper that her voice shook with it. 'I will. I think you found it easier. I think you're a rich and powerful man, Your

Highness. I think you didn't want your ship's cook getting the wrong ideas about your interest in her,' she flung at him.

His head went back as if she had hit him. The faint noise that she had been aware of became recognisable footsteps. They were getting closer. Neither Luc nor Christina paid any attention to them.

'I accept the snoops. I may not like it, but I'm not unreasonable. There were the children to consider. I accept that you had to have me investigated.'

Luc was very still. 'So?'

'What I don't accept is the lying,' Christina said flatly. 'The face-to-face, personal lying.'

He said evenly, 'What do you think would have happened if you had known who I was when we came face to face here?'

Christina set her teeth. 'Something more honest than what did happen.'

'That depends on your definition of honesty.'

'My definition is fairly standard,' she flashed.

He moved closer, bending his head to scan her face in the darkness. The space between their bodies was infinitesimal. She was trapped between him and the wooden wall behind her. Christina turned her head away sharply.

His voice level, Luc said, 'When my father died, I found out something that most people don't realise: a prince like me is a sort of actor. I can never forget that. There is the person I am talking to—and then all the rest, watching me talk to him. They're all watching for signs: signs I'm going to make wrong decisions because I'm angry or tired; signs I'm not going to make any decision at all because I'm out of my depth; signs I don't understand what is happening in my country or the rest of the world; signs of a weakness, any weakness, they can exploit to their advantage. So the Prince can't afford any anger or tiredness or bewilderment.' He paused, then added deliberately, 'Or weakness.'

Christina felt her anger falter. He sounded so sincere. But then, she reminded herself, hadn't he sounded sincere before?

'I didn't plan it. But when I arrived—you were so angry with the Prince. I thought, If she finds out who I am now, she'll never see me clearly again.'

He put out a gentle hand and brought her chin round to face him. She could see the gleam of his eyes in his shadowed face. She could feel her pulse hammering at the base of her throat.

'The Prince is a performance,' Luc told her quietly. 'I didn't want you to know the performance. I wanted you to know me.'

The anger had almost all gone. Only the hurt was left. He had asked her to go to bed with him. When would he have told her the truth? In the morning? At the end of the week? Ever?

'But I *didn't* know you, did I?' she said at last in a small voice. 'You took good care of that.'

He stared down at her, as if he could read her very soul. Her eyes fell under that penetrating scrutiny. The footsteps were louder, closer.

'Someone's coming,' Christina said, agitated.

Luc took no notice. 'Everything I ever told you was true,' he said in a low, urgent voice.

She closed her eyes. 'You've been playing diplomacy so long, you've forgotten how ordinary people see the truth. Everything you ever told me was to protect you in case I got too demanding.'

For a moment he was so still that she thought he had stopped breathing. She was so wretched herself that she felt as if she was in actual physical pain. She made a clumsy gesture, repudiating him. There was a silence like the end of the world.

Then Luc's arms fell. He stepped back.

At last he said very quietly, 'If you think that, there's no more to be said.'

Christina's eyes flew open. This was not what she'd expected. Suddenly he was not the Luc she knew. Even now she had more than half thought that he would shout at her and shake her and kiss her into submission, if that was what it took. In her most secret heart, that was almost what she wanted. This chilly dignity was unnerving.

'You—' she began.

But the footsteps were stamping down the companionway now. They stopped.

'Who's there?' shouted Captain Demetrius out of the darkness.

Luc turned and went to him without a backward look. 'Good evening, Captain,' he said in easy Greek.

The captain was less efficient than Simon. He had not brought a torch. He leaned forward over the handrail.

'Your Highness?' he said, incredulity in the brandy-slurred tones.

'As you see,' Luc said pleasantly, 'I was able to get away after all.'

She might never have existed. Christina watched his turned back. She could feel her skin getting colder and colder. I can't stand any more of this, she realised suddenly.

Unseen by Luc or the captain, she turned and slipped away into the dark.

She went to her cabin and locked the door decisively. Not that there was any reason for it. The last thing this new, cold Luc was going to do was come to her cabin. But still there was a satisfying symbolism in setting her shoulder to the rickety door and turning the key in the lock.

It was a long time before she lay down. Even longer before she slept. She heard the Princess return in the small hours. The crew were already back and gone to their quarters but someone met her. Wakeful on her bed, Christina heard muffled voices, a sharp protest from the Princess, the slam of a door.

So she was not the only one at odds with His impossible Highness, Christina thought wryly. The Princess suddenly had more of her sympathy than she had ever had before.

The next morning Christina was late and heavy-eyed. The captain and crew hardly spoke over their food. The family breakfast was not much better. The children were sulky and fidgeting. Luc was remote, absorbed in a file of papers. The Princess had retreated behind tinted glasses but she took them off to butter her toast. The puffy red eyelids told their own story.

The Princess grabbed her coffee as if it were the elixir of life and said in a bright, false voice, 'The party, Christina. Everything in hand?'

Luc did not look up. Out of the corner of her eye Christina saw his brows twitch together but to all intents and purposes he seemed absorbed in his reading.

'Yes, madam. Do you know how many are coming yet?'

'No. Now my brother has arrived to play the host we may need to change the guest list a little, of course,' the Princess said with an edge to her voice.

'Fine,' Christina said colourlessly.

Luc did look up at that. Christina felt his sharp inspection although she refused to acknowledge it. She knew that she was not looking her best. She had plaited her hair and pinned it on top of her head to keep it out of her way while she was cooking. The austere style made her face look too thin, her chin too pointed and, after a night like last night, her wide blue eyes huge and haunted. She hoped Luc did not think her wan appearance was because of him. But if he did there was not a thing she could do about it except pretend that he was not there.

She said, 'I'll be going to the market in an hour. Shall I take the children again, madam?'

'Would you like to go with Christina, darlings?'

'They'll spend the day with me.' Luc intervened before Simon or Pru could answer. 'You should come too, Marie Anne. We can go up the coast, swimming.'

Christina almost winced. Was he taking them to that little deserted cove?

'Perhaps Christina would like to come too?' he added.

'No,' she said on pure reflex.

It sounded rude. The Princess looked surprised. Luc's eyes narrowed.

She retrieved her mistake as best she could. 'I mean, there's too much to do getting the party ready.'

She gave a meaningless smile which embraced the whole table. Studiously avoiding Luc's smouldering eyes, she retreated.

Fortunately it was a busy day. After her shopping, she worked in the hot little galley until she thought she was going to collapse. She emerged only when summoned to the main deck.

The Princess was sitting in a sun-lounger looking shattered.

'What a day,' she said. 'I don't know what's got into Kay. I've never seen him like this.'

Christina bit her lip. 'I didn't know the Prince was back.'

'Well, he is. And snapping at everything in range.' The Princess took on a self-righteous expression. 'How was I to know he didn't want to see Juliette Legrain? I could hardly ask everyone else from the film and leave her out. Anyway, they were still an item the last I heard. He escorted her everywhere.'

'Oh,' said Christina hollowly. She tried to convince herself that she didn't care who the Prince escorted.

'But apparently they've broken up. So Kay's mad at me. I must say,' added the Princess darkly, 'I wonder if he's told Juliette.'

Christina shifted uncomfortably. 'Would you like something, madam?'

'What? Oh, yes, that's why I rang. Have you got any of that lemonade you made for the children? I'm parched.'

'I'll get it,' said Christina, glad to escape these unwelcome confidences.

But when she returned with an ice-rimmed jug and glasses her heart fell to her toes. The Prince was back.

He was standing four-square in front of his sister's lounger. She was looking up at him in trepidation. He acknowledged Christina's arrival with no more than an unsmiling look.

'My boat. My holiday. My family. My business,' Luc was saying. He sounded icy. 'My bodyguard has got better things to do than follow you round on your assignations with strange men.'

The Princess caught sight of Christina. She gave a nervous laugh.

'Oh, you mean the boy in the hotel pool. He isn't a strange man. He's the swimming instructor. He teaches the children. And he's Christina's boyfriend.'

'*What?*' Luc's face was suddenly grim.

About to deny it, Christina suddenly clamped her teeth shut on the words. It might be all to the good if Luc thought that Karl was more than a friend.

His sister gave Christina an apologetic, charming smile.

'In fact, he wanted me to give her a message. Sorry, I forgot, Christina. He was asking if you want to go to the hotel disco tonight. Call him if you want to. Er— what's his name?'

'Karl,' said Christina.

'Yes, of course. Karl. I'd forgotten.'

Luc was staring at Christina as if she had suddenly turned radioactive. Even his sister noticed.

'He seems very pleasant,' she added, her bright tone faltering.

Christina met Luc's eyes unflinchingly. 'He is.'

He made no movement. His expression told her nothing at all.

'Then of course you must go,' Luc said at last politely. He sounded as remote as the moon.

He was even more arctic when she came up onto deck that night before leaving to meet Karl. She was wearing a simple black shift, with gold chains at her throat. Luc's eyes swept her up and down, leaving her feeling as if she had been lightly dusted with frost.

'Have a good time,' said the Princess kindly.

Luc's smile was sardonic. 'Don't get carried away, Cinderella.'

Christina raised her brows. 'Is that an oblique way of telling me to be back before midnight?'

The handsome face closed. 'If that's how you want to take it.'

'Kay,' protested the Princess, startled.

But Christina gave him a glittering smile. She clicked her heels in their soft-soled pumps.

'Sir!' she said, sketching a salute.

For a moment she thought his mouth twitched. He touched her on the elbow. It was just a touch, no more. But it made her whole body jerk with awareness.

She removed her elbow at once before dancing off down the gangway with an airy wave. She hoped that Luc did not detect that her stylish exit was all too close to a retreat.

If she'd thought the evening would take her mind off Luc, she could not have been more wrong. Karl was glad to see her but throughout the evening he seemed more interested in hearing about her glamorous employer than he was in her, Christina noted wryly. The problem was that it was all to easy to talk about Luc. She liked Karl, she adored dancing and the disco was a good one. It made no difference. It was as if Luc were at her shoulder all the time.

In the end she gave up and asked Karl to take her home. He was friendly and attentive but he made no protest about leaving before midnight. Which was just as well, because she had come to the end of her ability to pretend to be enjoying herself.

He walked her back to the harbour.

'Will I see you again?'

'I don't know how long we're in port,' Christina said. 'There's a party tomorrow but after that I just don't know.'

'If the party finishes in time, call me. We can dance again,' he said. He sent her a sideways look. 'Or I could come and help out—wait tables, play the records.'

Christina was taken aback.

Karl grinned. 'If that will get me an invitation to meet the Prince,' he said frankly. 'He negotiated the Trakai Peace Treaty. To be honest, he's one of my heroes. My thesis is on twentieth-century localised wars. He could really help.'

'I'm glad he can help someone,' muttered Christina, but she was impressed in spite of herself. Aloud she said, 'OK, I'll see what I can do. Be in touch.'

Karl gave her waist a grateful squeeze. 'Thanks.'

He watched her onto the boat, then waved and turned back the way he had come. Pausing by the rail, Christina smiled ruefully at his retreating back.

Then her smile died. For all his interest in the Prince, Karl had not noticed how she'd tensed every time his name had been mentioned. But it was only a matter of time before somebody did, she thought. You couldn't go around feeling as if you were being launched into mid-air every time someone said a certain name without it showing on your face.

'Damn him,' she muttered. She was not talking about Karl.

She hesitated, looking round warily. There were lights on the other side of the boat and a couple of the state-rooms were still illuminated but there was no one on this side of the deck. More particularly, no Luc.

'Oh, for heaven's sake,' she said to herself. 'Are you a woman or a mop for him to wipe the floor with?'

That was better. Forget the way he made her heart faint with desire. Remember she was an independent woman. Remember she had sworn that she would never, like her poor mother, put her life on hold while she waited for the man of her dreams. Remember he had lied and lied even while he'd urged her to go to bed with him. Unfortunately, along with those salutary recollections came the less welcome one that she had very nearly gone with him.

'Damn,' said Christina.

Someone came round the corner. Christina's heart lurched up to her throat and fluttered there like a trapped moth. She stopped and drew herself up to her full height.

But it was not the Prince. As soon as she caught the smell of stale brandy on the air, she knew who it was. Christina stiffened, but she did not let her apprehension show.

'Good evening,' she said pleasantly.

'Good evening, *Captain*,' Demetrius corrected her. He sounded truculent, which was normal. He was also slurring his words, which was not.

Her apprehension grew.

'Good evening, Captain,' she replied in a level voice.

'You're back at last, then.' He added something slurred and insulting which Christina decided not to understand. In his turn, he decided to be more explicit. 'Got a man in the hotel, then?'

She tried to take it lightly. 'Several of them. And they're still dancing.'

He did not think that was funny. 'What's wrong with you? Don't you like men?'

He leaned forward, peering at her in the semi-dark. The brandy fumes were almost palpable. He did not frighten her but the smell was unpleasant. She took a couple of steps away from him.

'Some of my best friends are men,' she said neutrally.

'Friends! Pah!' He made a lurching grab for her which, between the brandy and the distorting effect of the shadows, came nowhere near her. 'You married?'

For some reason that made her wince. She did not understand it. Lots of people had asked her that over the last six years. It had never made her wince before.

But she answered steadily. 'No.'

'I am.'

Ah, so that was where he was heading. Here it comes, thought Christina resignedly. My wife doesn't understand me; I need someone to think I am wonderful. She braced herself.

But Captain Demetrius was more direct than she gave him credit for.

'I am. Married, I mean. Makes no difference. At sea, weeks apart. I do what I want. Know what I mean?'

'Yes,' said Christina grimly.

'I told you at start—'

'And I told you when I came on board that I was here to cook. Nothing else.'

He did not appear to have heard her. He made another grab. She evaded him easily but this time his hand touched her bare arm. She could not repress an exclamation—or her little shiver of distaste. He decided to misinterpret both.

'You be nice to me. We can make a good thing out of this trip.'

'This is as nice as I get,' Christina said.

He made his third grab. Christina had been on her own for six years. She knew how to look after herself. Captain Demetrius was strong but he was off balance and fuddled by the drink with which he had been drowning his embarrassing failures. She sidestepped him neatly, twisted out of the reach of his flailing arm and pushed him back hard against the bulkhead.

'Touch me again and I'll throw you,' she said evenly. 'I can you know. I'm on my third judo course.'

She could hear him breathing hard in the darkness, feel his eyes on her. Malice was as heavy in the air as the brandy fumes. He said nothing. But that didn't mean he wasn't feeling anything.

Christina bit her lip. It had not been a good trip for Captain Demetrius—accident upon accident, then one, public humiliation in front of the employer's sister and now another, private rejection at the hands of the lowest member of the crew. To a man of his temperament, that would probably be even more shaming. She would have to watch her step with him even more than she had done up to now.

She was making a resolve to do just that when she found it was too late. He grabbed her in a clumsy but powerful embrace. To her chagrin Christina, the accomplished brown belt, found it impossible to remove herself. He was breathing hard, fumbling with her short, full skirt. Christina felt his bruising grip on her upper thigh and abandoned the principles of a lifetime.

She put back her head and yelled for help.

CHAPTER EIGHT

CHRISTINA'S assailant swore virulently and clamped a hand over her mouth. She bit him. He jumped and his hold loosened involuntarily. She hooked a foot round his ankle and nearly overbalanced him. But for all Demetrius's brandy-induced swaying he had a perverse ability to stay on his feet. She fought strenuously, her hair flying.

And then abruptly he let her go. Christina was not expecting it and she half fell to the deck, ending on one knee. Her chest rose and fell agonisingly with the effort to steady her breathing. She did not know what had happened.

She shook her head to clear it. She looked up.

Captain Demetrius was backed up against the iron stairway. The expression of dismay on his face was almost comical. His opponent was tall, but slim as a whip. It was not his size which set the burly captain cowering, a shaken Christina thought, but the stark rage which came off him in waves.

'Y-your Highness...I can explain...' he began thickly.

Luc cut him off with an abrupt gesture, like a razor slicing through the air. Demetrius flinched.

'Enough.'

Christina hauled herself to her feet. The captain's eyes slid round his opponent to her.

'This little tramp was back late,' he said virtuously. 'She is no good. No good. It is her fault we collide with the other boat. And when we do she laughs. *Laughs*.'

'I heard,' said Luc.

135

Christina thought that if she had been the captain the ice in that soft voice would have frozen her to the spot. Demetrius, however, did not notice.

'It is my responsibility to discipline the crew. I am Captain.'

Saying it seemed to give him confidence. His shoulders straightened. Luc surveyed him with an expression that made Christina quail.

'Not on any boat of mine,' he said softly.

The captain stared as if he did not understand.

'I have had enough, by God I have,' Luc said with sudden harshness. 'The boat is damaged. The cruise is a shambles. The harbour-master would have prosecuted if Christina hadn't talked him out of it.'

He glanced briefly, coldly at Christina. Her presence clearly reminded him of yet another cause of displeasure.

'That galley is lethal. As captain you are, as you have pointed out, responsible. And I do not care for your methods of disciplining female crew members. You will leave tomorrow.'

Captain Demetrius was clearly trying to overcome the effect of the brandy fumes. He shook his head. 'I have a contract...' he challenged.

'You will be paid.' Luc said. 'Come to my office at eight. You shall have all the money your contract specifies. And then I want you off this boat by nine tomorrow morning. Is that clear?'

'You can't do that...' the captain began to bluster.

Luc was implacable. 'I assure you I can.'

'Because of one little tramp?' He was incredulous.

Luc hit him.

The blow finally knocked the captain off his precarious balance. He slid down the wall behind him, an expression of the blankest astonishment on his face. He put the back of his hand to his mouth. His lip was bleeding.

'I'll sue,' he said triumphantly.

Luc was not even breathing heavily. He reached out
a long arm, gathered together a fistful of the man's
T-shirt and hauled him onto his feet.

'Understand me, Captain Demetrius. You collect your
money and leave tomorrow, or you will be removed.'

'You wouldn't call the police.'

'Who said anything about the police?'

Luc's teeth gleamed white. He was smiling like a jaguar
sighting its prey, thought Christina with a shudder.

'So far I haven't had much of a holiday, Captain
Demetrius,' he said conversationally. 'Removing you
personally from my vicinity might just change that.'

The captain peered at Luc. Whatever he saw in his
face clearly convinced him that the prudent course was
to accede.

'I get all my pay?'

'You have my word.'

The captain shrugged. 'OK. Your loss.'

Luc released his shirt. Demetrius shook himself,
smoothed his grubby T-shirt and left with as much
dignity as he could manage in the circumstances. Luc
watched him go.

'Did he hurt you?' he flung over his shoulder at
Christina at last. He did not look at her.

She was shaken by the ugly little scene.

'No. He—startled me, that's all.'

Luc did look at her then. 'Say terrified and you'd be
nearer the mark. I heard you scream. He frightened you,
didn't he?'

Her dignity was outraged. 'No. I can take care of
myself.'

Luc reached out and flicked at the torn strap of her
dress.

'So I see,' he said ironically.

She blushed and grabbed a hand to it. The strap had
slipped disastrously, exposing far too much of a creamy

breast. Luc watched, his eyes hooded. She glared at him
in defiance. Abruptly he turned away.

'It cannot go on. But this is not the time to discuss
it.'

Christina gave a hard laugh. 'Does that mean you want
me to see you in your office tomorrow as well?'

He stiffened. 'That is an idea, certainly,' he said evenly.

She prowled round and stood in front of him, her chin
thrust forward challengingly.

'Are you going to sack me too, Your Highness?' she
mocked. Her heart twisted with pain but she ignored it.

At his side his hand clenched slowly. Christina saw it
and was perversely triumphant. At least it meant that
his demeanour of princely cool was costing him something in self-restraint. A desire to blast him out of it
took hold of her.

Afterwards she could hardly believe what she did next.
It had to have been the shock of the fight.

She smiled, and quite deliberately let the torn strap
of her dress fall. She held his eyes.

For a moment Luc stood as if turned to stone. Then
Christina saw that the tell-tale muscle was working un-
controllably below his cheekbone. Success, she thought
without compunction.

But he gave no other sign of reaction. And when he
spoke his voice was so cool that it was almost bored.
'Sacking you certainly has its attractions. But this is really
not the time. I will see you in the morning.'

He walked quickly away before she could say any
more. Christina stared after him in disbelief. He couldn't
just walk away from her like that. He *couldn't*.

Oh, she hated Luc Henri, Prince of Kholkhastan, as
she had never hated anyone in her cool and self-possessed
life. She hated him.

It was not a good night. She was up early, making waffles
to give her something to take her mind off the forth-

coming interview. The children were delighted but the Princess looked very much as Christina felt.

'I didn't think it could, but Kay's mood has got *worse*,' she said gloomily. 'It could be the accident with the boat, I suppose. He made us all tell him about it last night after you'd gone. It was like some policeman taking statements. He was *furious*. Now he says we can't stay on the boat!'

So when Christina went to the room that Luc had made his study she expected to be paid off, just like the captain.

She knocked and went in when bidden. Luc was looking at a leather-bound folder, marking something. She caught the flash of gold as he recapped his pen. He looked up as soon as she came in and closed the folder.

He was wearing his suit again, which was lightweight and beautifully cut, offset by a marvellous silk tie. How could I ever have thought he was a gossip columnist? Christina thought. He looked every inch the international negotiator—and as remote as the moon.

'Good morning, Christina,' he said with grave courtesy. 'I hope you slept well.'

She was instantly on the defensive. 'Why shouldn't I?'

'You were up exceptionally early,' he pointed out wryly. 'As I was myself,' he added deliberately.

Christina's eyes narrowed. Was he trying to tell her something? Surely not that his dreams were as disturbingly full of her as hers were of him? It would have been some comfort, perhaps, but it was hardly likely. She dismissed the suspicion as soon as it occurred to her.

Instead she looked away, shrugging. She thought he sighed faintly. But when he spoke his voice was brisk.

'I have decided that we will continue our holiday ashore. The crew is incompetent and I really have not the time to engage another one. Besides, the boat needs a good deal of work done. I shall be arranging it today.

My sister will have her party tonight. After that we will all go to a villa I own further along the coast.'

'I see.'

It was what she had expected but it still hurt, especially as he had not excluded her from the crew he called incompetent. But she was not going to let him see it.

She lifted her chin. 'I take it I get my wages and my passage back to Athens.'

He frowned. 'I would prefer you to come with us.'

Christina stared. 'Hasn't this villa got a cook?' she said incredulously.

'It has a full complement of domestic staff but I want you to take care of the children. They will need someone to oversee their amusements.'

'I'm not a nanny.'

'Are you refusing?'

She met his eyes. She could not read anything in the expression on the handsome face.

He said coolly, 'I see from the contract you signed that we have the use of your services for another ten days. It does not actually specify your tasks. I would prefer you to work the rest of your employment at the Villa San Bernardino. That is all.'

'But—'

'Christina, when does your next job start?' he said patiently.

She was so disconcerted that she answered him literally. 'Two days after I get back. Oh!'

'Precisely. If you run out on us you will have to go and sleep on the floor of your long-suffering friend,' he said with a ghost of a smile. 'Is that fair—twice in as many months?'

She had to admit that there was something in what he said, even though it went against the grain.

'The children won't be a nuisance,' he said. 'I know Simon has not been easy. It is not altogether his fault.'

He hesitated before adding in a dry tone, 'I am sure you will have realised that all is not well between his parents. I have now told my brother-in-law that his marriage and his family are *his* problems and he has to sort them out. He will be with us tonight or tomorrow. So Simon's behaviour should improve dramatically.' He paused. 'Well?'

Christina bit her lip. All she wanted to do was get away from Luc Henri in this alienating royal guise, she assured herself. So why was she trying to find reasons— no, not reasons, excuses—for staying in his employment?

He said softly, 'Be sensible, Christina. Even if you hate the very idea, it's hardly for ever. What is ten days out of your life, after all?'

But she didn't hate the very idea. That was the trouble. Christina decided that there was no point in pretending. Squaring her shoulders, she looked him in the eyes and said, 'And what about you and me?'

She had surprised Luc, she saw. For a moment the cool mask twitched in shock. Then he clamped down on whatever he was feeling. He was cool and expressionless again.

He said carefully, 'That is a separate issue.'

Christina was incredulous. 'You mean you're going to pretend none of it happened?'

'Nothing very much has happened,' he pointed out. 'A couple of kisses. A lot of misunderstanding. That's it.'

A couple of kisses. That was all they were to him? Yet they had turned her world upside down. Christina could have hit him.

'You needn't worry that I shall pursue the matter against your will,' he went on.

From his tone he could have been talking about some boring but not very important subject on the international agenda. Or a business deal, Christina thought grimly.

'Good,' she agreed.

'Then that's settled.'

Christina realised that she had been manipulated by a master. Without actually agreeing to do what he wanted, she had tacitly accepted that she would. If only it wasn't, in her heart of hearts, what she wanted too— to be with him, she thought, she would stamp out and hitch a ride back to Athens now.

Luc turned away, clearly dismissing her now that he had won his point.

'Please be packed and ready by midday tomorrow. I am glad you will be joining us at the villa. I hope you will enjoy it,' he said formally.

Christina's manners were not as good as his. Or maybe it was because she had not had years of training in disguising her emotions. She glared. Then she turned on her heel and went out of the cabin without a word. She even banged the door behind her.

If she had expected Luc to come after her in some attempt at reconciliation, she was disappointed. Almost as soon as she had banged out, he left the yacht.

'Will His Highness be back for the party?' Christina asked the Princess when she served lunch.

'He'll be back all right,' said his sister grimly. 'How else is he going to keep an eye on me?'

Christina prudently did not answer that one, though she sympathised. Instead, mindful of her promise to Karl, she said, 'The guest list has increased so much— do you think it would be an idea to hire someone apart from me to hand round drinks?'

The Princess was supremely uninterested. 'Go ahead.'

Christina did not have time to go ashore again but she called the hotel on the mobile phone. Karl was nearly incoherent with gratitude.

'I'll remember you in my will,' he promised.

'Just turn up looking like a waiter, not a surfer,' Christina begged.

She could hear his grin down the phone. 'You got it.'

Karl did indeed look remarkably tidy and sober when he arrived in dark trousers and a waist-length white jacket borrowed from one of the waiters at his hotel. It set off his tan. With his flowing hair clipped into a neat queue at the back of his neck, he looked positively handsome. A number of the female guests paid him more than passing attention, Christina saw.

The trouble was that Luc saw it too. He had returned late from wherever he had been and disappeared immediately to change for the party. The first time Christina caught sight of him he was observing Karl narrowly. His expression was forbidding.

Perhaps it was because his own companion was one of those who had shown her appreciation of Karl's athletic presence, Christina thought. It was a painful reflection but she could not dismiss it. Stuart Define had come on board accompanied by his glamorous co-star.

As soon as she saw Luc, Juliette Legrain detached herself from the actor and took up residence at Luc's side. Christina heard her shrieks of delight even though she could not see her over the heads of the other guests. As soon as she could see them, she found Luc was looking down into the beautiful, vivid face with undisguised affection.

He never looked at me like that, Christina thought with an odd little stab of pain under her heart. For a moment the tray of exquisite canapés tilted dangerously. She looked down, shaken by the strength of her feelings. She righted it at once and resumed circulating among the guests. But she felt dazed—as if something about seeing Luc arm-in-arm with Juliette Legrain had the effect of a blow on the head.

What is wrong with me? Christina peered at the cracked mirror in the galley. She was too busy for self-analysis but she still could not get it out of her head that something momentous had happened. In spite of the warmth of the Italian night, and the lights and companionable noise of conversation on deck, Christina felt as if she was somewhere dark and cold and empty. She had never felt so alone in her entire life.

Eventually the party was down to a few assorted stragglers. Luc dealt competently with them while the family congregated in the stateroom. The Princess came down to the galley. Karl leaped to his feet politely. In spite of her strange detached feeling, Christina straightened.

'Dinner?' she asked professionally.

The Princess looked faintly horrified. 'Good heavens, no. You've done quite enough work for one evening. Kay and I will take everyone out for a meal,' she said. 'I'm just going to organise a table now.'

Behind her shoulder Luc appeared. He was looking coolly, elegantly in control, just as he had all evening.

'I hope you will be able to join us,' he said to Christina with distant courtesy.

It did not sound like an invitation. It sounded like an order. Christina could not find anything to say. The silence became embarrassing.

The Princess looked startled but she said quickly, 'Christina must be exhausted—'

'Not too exhausted to eat,' Luc said flatly.

Yes, definitely an order. Christina stared at him in indignation. 'There's a lot of clearing up to do...' she began.

But Karl had seen the chance of a real opportunity to question his hero. 'I'll help. It won't take long,' he said eagerly. 'We could be ready in fifteen minutes.'

There was a sharp little silence. Luc's eyes flickered.

If Karl had not been an obsessional student he would have noticed that there was no rush to include him in the invitation. But he did not. He just said he would start by getting the dirty glasses from the upper deck. He went.

The Princess sent her brother a speculative look. 'He is so helpful, isn't he? You must bring him along too, of course, Christina.'

Luc said nothing. There was a small, nasty pause. Then the Princess announced that she would go and call a restaurant and followed Karl.

Left alone with Luc, Christina busied herself with the dishes. She could feel him watching her but he said nothing. She did not look at him.

At last he said in a curt voice, 'My sister tells me the boy is a particular friend of yours.'

Christina did not look round. She shrugged, stacking glasses.

'Is it true?'

She straightened then and turned to face him. 'I've known him a long time.'

Luc's smile slashed into his think cheek. It did not reach his eyes. 'By which you mean several summers, I take it. You play together in the sun before going your own way, isn't that it?' He sounded angry.

'There isn't a lot of call for my sort of crewing in the winter,' Christina agreed levelly.

'Does he know where you go in the winter?' Luc shot at her suddenly.

Momentarily Christina was blank. 'What?'

'Nobody else seems to.'

She looked at him in dawning comprehension. Indignation sparked. 'Your private detective still on the case?' she enquired with dangerous pleasantness.

Luc's smile was equally dangerous. When he spoke it was in his official voice, reporting facts without emotion. 'He got as far as Milan. Then he said it was a wall. No address, just a post office box. No employer. No regular associates.'

Christina gave sudden thanks for her itinerant studentship. She had never had any reason to cover her tracks but it was a small triumph that there was something at least in which she could get the better of the Prince of Kholkhastan.

'Frustrating,' she observed politely.

Luc's eyes bored into her. 'Well?'

Christina braced herself against the sink behind her and faced him squarely. 'I work for you for another ten days,' she said. 'Then I'm gone.'

'That's not good enough.'

'Oh, but it is,' she flashed. 'You've done your best to turn my life upside down from the moment I met you. You have no scruples at all. It's only the merest chance that—'

She broke off. She had been going to say that it was only by chance that she had not made love to him when he'd set out so blatantly to seduce her. But from the way his eyes gleamed suddenly she realised that that was exactly what he expected her to say. Wanted her to say.

So she wouldn't.

Instead she finished carefully, 'That I haven't been badly hurt by all your lies.'

In spite of his cool command of himself he flinched at that. Christina saw it and felt better.

'When I leave your employment I want to be very certain that you have no way of finding me ever again,' she told him flatly.

Luc's eyes darkened. He stood there for a moment, not speaking. Then suddenly he gave a quick, angry grimace and turned on his heel.

As the door closed behind him, Christina let out a long breath that she did not even know she had been holding. She felt she had won some obscure battle that she had not realised she had been fighting. She also felt the war was not over.

For the rest of the evening, however, Luc did not come near her. The restaurant was a jolly, informal affair, with tables set outside under a vine. The Princess had taken the precaution of asking Karl herself. Unaware of the tensions, he sat next to her, thoroughly enjoying himself. The Princess seemed to know a good many of the diners at the other tables. As a result, the comings and goings between the tables was enough to disguise the fact that Luc neither looked at Christina nor spoke to her. He spoke to Karl, though, at length.

In fact, after an initial chilly hauteur, he seemed rather to take to Karl, Christina saw. The power of flattery, she thought cynically. Presumably Karl had told Luc about his thesis. He must have been flattered to find himself figuring as the hero of an academic study.

Karl was quite simply delighted. It made her feel excluded, but she disguised it when she said goodnight to Karl.

'Thank you for your help at the party,' she said, giving him a quick kiss. 'I hope the Prince lived up to expectations.'

Karl hugged her. 'He did, he did. In fact he's promised me more. Exclusive stuff. This thesis could turn into a full-scale book.' He grinned. 'My writing career is about to begin, thanks to you.'

'I'm glad.'

'You'd better let me know where to send you a copy when it's finished. Autographed, of course.'

'Of course,' Christina said, laughing.

She told him her address in Milan. He looked disappointed.

'But that's a box number.'

'I travel a lot,' she said. 'It's safer waiting at the post office to be claimed.'

'Well, give me a phone number at least. I might come through Milan on my great lecture tour. When the book is published the universities of the world are going to be clamouring for me,' Karl said complacently.

Christina shook her head at his vanity but gave him the number of the flat in Milan. When she was away she called in every day to pick up the messages on her answering machine. He scribbled it down in a battered address book.

'Thanks. I'll definitely call you, even if I don't make the best-seller lists,' Karl said. He gave her a swift hug. 'Look after yourself. Kay is a great guy.'

He went before Christina could ask what he meant by that odd rider. Eventually she concluded that sheer exuberance at getting the interview he wanted had made him chatter. She had known Karl through enough summer seasons to know that nothing was as important to him as his university career.

She could not quite put the final remark of his out of her mind, though. Several times during the busy preparations of the next morning she came within a whisker of demanding an explanation from Luc. Was it only his UN experience that he had talked about to Karl?

But in the end she stayed away from Luc. He was busier than any of them, with his telephone and fax. He looked remote and somehow curbed, as if it would take very little for him to explode into a truly terrible temper. Christina thought it was definitely better to avoid him in that mood. She watched the Princess and the children walking carefully round him and decided that she was not the only one who sensed the impending explosion either.

They got to the villa without mishap. Well, it was not so much a villa, more a medieval castle with palatial additions, she saw wryly. There was even an older statesman of a butler in what she took to be Kholkhastani dress presiding over the household. As she had expected, the staff was plentiful and efficient. She was going to be wholly superfluous. She did approach Luc then.

'You don't need me here,' she said. 'You know you don't. Why don't I just go back to Athens?'

He fixed her with a glare like a laser.

'You manifestly don't know what I need.' Luc's voice was level but his eyes glittered dangerously.

They were in his study, surrounded by a strange mixture of ancient, leather-bound books and modern computer hardware. She had interrupted him at his work. He looked up from his desk, his face thin with suppressed emotion of some kind.

Or maybe it was just exhaustion. Although she had only known him as the Prince for three days, Christina was already appalled by the amount of work he seemed to do. He was still a lying, unscrupulous seducer, of course, but she was revising her other earlier opinions. This was no playboy.

Which made his dealings with her all the more incomprehensible. And unforgivable, she assured herself.

'Why don't you admit it? I'm here just because once you've taken somebody onto the payroll you just have to get every last minute of work in the contract out of them,' she flashed.

A wintry amusement invaded his expression. 'You really don't think much of me at all, do you, Christina?'

'I tell things the way I see them,' she said sturdily.

He was thoughtful. 'Not much of me. Not much of yourself.'

She shook her head violently. 'That's not true. I'm happy with who I am. The only thing I'm unhappy about is dictatorial strangers telling me what's wrong with me.'

His mouth tilted. 'I'll be happy to explore the matter— but at some future date, I'm afraid. There are things which need my attention now.'

Christina could have stamped her foot. She only refrained because it would have deepened his amusement. She went to the door but turned in the doorway for a parting shot. 'I will be wasting my time here. And you know it.'

He gave a soft laugh. 'That depends on what you mean by wasting your time. With a bit of give and take, it could be quite productive.'

Christina's pulses leaped. She calmed them. 'I will not be doing the giving,' she announced, nose in the air.

His amusement died. 'Tell me something I don't know.'

The telephone beside him rang. He picked it up at once. 'Yes? Oh, it's you, Richard. About time.'

He gave a nod of dismissal to Christina. She went, half-relieved, half-frustrated.

As she closed the door behind her, she heard him say grimly, 'I appreciate that but I have my own life, you know. It's in serious need of my attention just at the moment.'

Christina went in search of the Princess. Since she was ostensibly there to take care of the children, she would demonstrate that there was not a job for her by appealing to their mother.

The Princess was walking up and down on a colonnaded terrace which overlooked a formal garden full of fountains. She was talking to the butler. In his white trousers and high-necked jacket he looked serene and supremely distinguished. The Princess looked worried.

'Oh, there you are, Christina,' she said.

Her companion turned and bowed courteously. But Christina had the impression that he was not entirely pleased.

The Princess was oblivious. 'Simon seems to have taken off,' she said abruptly. 'You haven't seen him, have you?'

'Not since we arrived. He said he was going to swim,' said Christina, puzzled.

The Princess's frown intensified. 'That's what I thought too, but Sir Goraev—' She indicated the elderly butler '—says there's no one at the pool. And I know he's not in his room because I looked.'

Christina looked at the green landscape stretching down the hill in formal gardens and lemon groves. It shimmered in the afternoon sun. The bark of the olive trees looked almost silver; the lemon-tree leaves turned to gold where the sun reflected off them. It was idyllic.

'Perhaps he's gone for a walk.'

The Princess looked as if she was going to cry.

Sir Goraev said, 'He knows it is not permitted. There is a lot of land slippage on the hillside. Also—well, we have received no threats, thank God, but this is the country of political kidnap.'

The Princess shuddered, but she said sharply, 'Don't be so pessimistic, Sir Goraev. Kidnappers would have no interest in an ordinary English boy.'

He bowed his head politely but was patently unconvinced. 'We must not forget he is also the nephew of His Highness.'

'We must not forget, either, that we have received no threats. Or that he is a disobedient little toad with no common sense at all,' said his fond mother with asperity. 'He's much more likely to have caught his foot in a rabbit hole. The first thing is to get the gardeners to search the woods. And tell my brother.'

Sir Goraev bowed. 'His Highness cannot be disturbed at the moment. I will inform him when he is at leisure.'

'But—'

'He is speaking to Kholkhastan,' he said with finality.

The Princess looked mutinous. But she did not argue. 'Very well, then. Organise a couple of search parties and then report back to me,' she said curtly.

He bowed again and left the terrace in a stately manner. The Princess glowered after him.

'That man gets more and more insufferable,' she muttered. 'If I were Kay, I'd sack him.'

Christina was startled at the venom in her voice. 'Who is he? I remember Pru telling me he ran things. I thought he was a sort of butler,' she confessed.

The Princess gave a harsh laugh. 'If only he were. No, he's more of a Lord Chamberlain, I suppose. When my grandfather was ill, Goraev developed a lot of power in Kholkhastan. He's trying to hold onto it. As soon as Kay went home, Goraev moved in on him, telling him what to do, who to see, what to say.

'I can't stand it. Kay's been an international negotiator all his working life. He knows more about diplomacy than Goraev ever will. He could have pensioned him off but he was too kind. So the old man even comes on private holidays like this, reminding Kay of work all the time. He never has any fun any more. It's all duty, duty, duty. It makes me mad.'

'His Highness certainly seems to work very hard,' Christina agreed neutrally.

'Too hard. What he needs is to get rid of all the ceremony nonsense and find himself a wife and a few children. That would give him a normal perspective again.' The Princess propped herself against one of the columns, looking down the heat-misted valley. 'Oh, where is Simon?' she burst out.

'He seems to know the place very well,' said Christina, who had sat next to Simon during the drive and listened to his tales of former holidays at the villa. 'Surely he couldn't get lost?'

The Princess bit her lip.

'Not by accident.' She sent Christina a quick look. 'He's been in a bit of a mood.'

Christina interpreted. 'You mean he could have run away?'

'I don't know. I don't know.' The other woman turned away suddenly, wringing her hands. 'I wish I could just *talk* to Kay.'

Christina said soothingly, 'If the gardeners are searching, they'll know the terrain better than His Highness, surely?'

'Oh, the terrain.' The Princess shrugged dismissively. 'Simon listens to Kay.' She hesitated, the exquisitely made-up face twisted. Then she went on in a burst, as if she could not help herself, 'I'm probably not telling you anything you haven't worked out for yourself. His father and I have had difficulties. The last couple of years Richard has become absolutely obsessed with work. We never saw him, so I gave him an ultimatum. Unfortunately Simon overheard and managed to convince himself that I was having an affair. He became completely unmanageable. I was truly grateful when Kay suggested the cruise. But everything went wrong right from the start.'

'Do you think your brother might know where Simon has gone?'

'I don't know that either. I just— Kay seems so much closer to him than I am at the moment.'

The Princess looked so wretched that Christina's determination not to get involved collapsed.

'Then let's ask him,' she said decisively.

'Sir Goraev won't let me anywhere near him.'

'There's two of us,' pointed out Christina. 'He won't be physically able to keep both of us at bay at the same time.'

The Princess stared at her. 'You mean it,' she said at last.

'Of course.'

'Kay would be very angry,' said his sister, with a shudder.

'Tough.'

The Princess eyed her with new respect. 'Don't you care if he's angry with you?'

'I'll survive.' Christina did not add, I have so far. Instead she took the other woman's arm. 'Come on. The sooner we get your brother involved, the sooner your mind will be at rest.'

This time when Christina went into his office Luc was standing by his desk in front of the window, the telephone under his ear, an expression of controlled exasperation on his face. There was no change when they flung open the door. His concentration was entirely on the subject in hand.

Sir Goraev was standing at the desk, sorting papers. When he saw them, he looked as exasperated as Luc and a good deal less controlled about it. He came over to them at once and stood between them and Luc.

'I regret but—'

The Princess said, 'Please . . .'

His expression was unyielding. Christina's simmering anger went to white heat. She pulled back and then darted past him, just as she had in long-ago playgrounds, before Sir Goraev had assimilated the fact that she was not going to do what he'd told her to. He muttered an expletive and reached for her but it was too late. She was down the long, book-lined room like a champion sprinter.

She put both hands on the desk and leaned across it, looking Luc compellingly in the eye, ignoring his telephone conversation.

'Simon is missing,' she said clearly.

His eyes flickered.

He said into the telephone, 'Then take it to the council. I have more important things to do,' and cut off the call.

There was absolute silence. Then the Princess drew an audible breath. She looked shaken.

'Explain,' Luc rapped out.

They all began to speak. He flung up a hand. They stopped.

'Christina, what has happened to my nephew?'

He's blaming me already, she thought. Because I said they didn't need looking after and now this happens. But she did not defend herself. There was no time.

'He's not in the house. He said he was going to swim but he hasn't been to the pool.'

Luc considered this. 'Run away?'

Sir Goraev said, 'The gardeners are searching. Now, you really need to consider the French proposal by tonight...'

Luc ignored him. 'Where is Pru?'

Christina jumped. 'She went to see the goats being milked.'

Luc sent her a look of irony. 'No, she didn't.'

'But—'

'Goats don't get milked in the middle of the day. The children have conned you.'

Christina flushed guiltily. He turned to his sister.

'I'd say they've taken to the woods together,' he said crisply. 'Knowing Simon, he will have worked out some ultimatum or other.'

'Then he will no doubt let us know in the course of time,' said Sir Goraev. 'Now, Your Highness, the French estimate—'

'You can't just leave it like that,' Christina cried. 'Woods can be dangerous for children. They could fall into a gully or there could be a landslip or—or anything. You can't just leave them out there without even trying to find them. They're *children* for God's sake.'

'As I've said, the gardeners are already searching for them. His Highness has higher responsibilities.' The old adviser turned back to Luc. 'Your duty, sir...'

Luc was watching Christina.

'Duty?' he said. 'Do I not also have a duty to my family, Goraev? To my feelings?'

There was something in his eyes that made Christina feel suddenly as if she was standing in a high wind with no support within reach. It was rather scary—but exhilarating.

'Of course you do,' she said. She was oddly breathless.

'Then for once, Goraev, old friend, I am listening to my feelings.'

'Your Highness—'

'Get the staff together in the kitchen,' Luc said to Christina. 'Including any of the gardeners that have not already started to search. I'm going to find my nephew.'

His eyes were brilliant. They never left Christina's face.

'And then I'm going to deal with other more important matters,' he said softly. 'Matters I have neglected for too long.'

CHAPTER NINE

Luc was right. Simon had left an ultimatum. Christina found it in his room on top of his unopened suitcase. She caught it up and ran out onto the landing, calling Luc's name.

At once he came up the stairs two at a time. 'You've found him?'

She held out the note silently. He tore it open and scanned it rapidly. Then he looked up. 'It could be worse. Simon says he and Pru won't come back to the villa until his father comes,' Luc reported.

Christina's eyes narrowed. 'How will he know? Will someone in the house tell him?'

Luc was frowning. 'Unlikely. I imagine he will go up to the ridge and watch the road.'

'The ridge? But surely...?'

He nodded. 'Where the landslips occurred. Dangerous. We must find them before they hurt themselves.'

Christina felt sick. 'This is my fault. I was so certain that you'd only got me here because you can't bear to be crossed. I never even tried to take care of the children. I knew Simon was unhappy. I just didn't *think*.'

In spite of his preoccupation, Luc touched her reassuringly on the shoulder.

'We all knew Simon was unhappy. None of us thought of this. You mustn't blame yourself.'

'But—'

'Christina.'

She stopped, her eyes swimming in tears. He put out a finger and tipped one very gently off her eyelashes. With a slanting smile he mocked himself. For the first

157

time since she had known that he was the Prince of Kholkhastan, Luc looked like the man she had met in Athens.

'Don't tear yourself to pieces,' he said gently. 'You're wrong about why I brought you here. But you're right, it wasn't to look after my nephew and niece.'

She was so worried about Simon that she could not even rouse any anger at his duplicity.

'What—?'

'This isn't the time to talk about it.' Then, as if he could not help himself, Luc feathered a caress under her damp lashes. His voice roughened. 'When I get back— this time I promise you the whole truth. Nothing prettied up. Nothing left out, God help me.'

Christina stared. There was an air of determination about him, as if he had set himself some vital and near impossible task.

'And you'd better do the same. Or I won't be answerable for the consequences.'

Before she could think of an answer, he had turned and gone back to the anxious Princess. Christina followed more slowly. Her thoughts were in turmoil.

Downstairs, Luc was calmly reassuring to his sister. However, Christina helped with his preparations to go in search of the children and noted that he included a strong climbing rope and a lightweight blanket that folded up into nothing.

'You think the children have had an accident?' she asked under her voice, helping him on with his pack.

Luc hesitated. Then he said low enough not to be overheard, 'It's possible. They took off as soon as they got here. Simon had no opportunity to reconnoitre. There may be new hazards since he was last here.'

Christina bit her lip. 'How dangerous is it? For you, I mean?'

Luc sent her a quick, surprised look. 'I learned my hill-walking skills in the Himalayas.'

'Oh.' She subsided, flushing, feeling foolish.

He touched her cheek briefly. 'But it's kind of you to worry.'

Her head reared up. 'I'm not worried. It's nothing to do with me what risks you run.'

Luc gave a soft laugh. 'How wrong you are.'

'I don't know what you're talking about,' Christina said crossly.

His eyes were dancing. But behind the look of mischief there was the determination that she had sensed upstairs.

'I'll make a deal with you. Wait for me and I'll explain.'

'Wait—?'

'It may take some time to find the children. Don't take off till I come back.'

'Of course not,' said Christina, outraged at the suggestion that she could be so hard-hearted. 'I couldn't leave the Princess at a time like this.'

Luc nodded. 'That's put me in my place,' he remarked. 'Fine. Stay and hold her hand. My brother-in-law will be grateful not to have a hysteric on his hands when he arrives, I've no doubt.'

Christina started. 'He's coming after all?'

'He was on his way before Simon staged his dramatic blackmail attempt,' he said dully. 'So you'd better get used to calling my sister Mrs Aston.' His mouth tilted suddenly in a wicked smile. 'On second thoughts, don't bother.' He settled his pack comfortably and went to the door. 'And don't run away,' he flung over his shoulder.

The afternoon wore into evening and none of the search party came back. The Princess insisted that Christina swim but she did not do so herself, jumping up at every sound. Sir Goraev joined them and made no secret of his disapproval.

'His Highness should not be distracted in this way,' he said. 'He has important decisions to make. He should be allowed to concentrate on them.' He looked with austere displeasure at Christina's tanned limbs as she climbed out of the swimming pool in her bikini.

The Princess gave a crack of rather high-pitched laughter. 'Christina hasn't been distracting him. If you don't like him being human, you should complain to Juliette Legrain.'

Christina hid her winces in the vigorous towelling she gave her hair. Of course, she had seen for herself how close they still were only the evening before. So why did she hate to hear the Princess confirm it?

I don't care what he does, she told herself, marching back to her room to change. I don't. This is just a passing attraction and I will get over it. I *will*. I don't care what it is he thinks he's going to do when he gets back. I'm not going to let him hurt me again. I shall just not think about him.

But as the night closed in it became increasingly difficult to think of anything else. One by one other members of the search party came back. But of the children and their uncles there was no sign.

Neither the Princess nor Christina managed more than a mouthful of any of the delicious four courses provided for their dinner. Even when her husband arrived, just as the coffee was being served, the Princess's welcome was muted. At first Richard Aston looked rather put out, but when she told him about the children being missing he looked aghast.

'Kay's gone looking for them and he's still not back? I'm going after him. Didn't it occur to you that he might be hurt? It's not just children who break their ankles in rabbit holes,' he said contemptuously.

'But Kay's so fit—'

'When he isn't working sixteen hours a day,' said Richard Aston grimly. 'These days, though...'

Christina thought of the powerful crawl that had taken Luc far out into the bay during their afternoon together, before she'd known who he was and her whole world had turned upside down.

She said unwarily, 'Don't worry. He's very fit.'

Husband and wife stared at her.

She flushed scarlet and stammered, 'I—I mean, I think he is. We swam, you see. A few days ago. He beat me easily and I'm a good swimmer.'

She lapsed into uncomfortable silence under Richard Aston's shrewd stare. His wife looked shattered. There was an embarrassing pause.

Sir Goraev said, 'I think I hear someone now.'

They all strained their ears. From the tiled corridors of the kitchen quarters came the unmistakable sound of Simon Aston announcing that he was all right.

'Simon,' sobbed his mother, and ran.

The two men followed. Christina got up from the table more slowly. Her face still felt hot. She cursed herself for an idiot, feeling as if she had betrayed herself. She went reluctantly to the top of the staircase, only to hear Luc's voice issuing equally unmistakable commands.

She sagged against the ornate banister. He was safe. He was *safe*. Relief and gladness swept through her. She began to run down the stairs towards his voice.

And stopped. What was she doing? She had no right to run to greet him. She was not a member of the family. She was not even a trusted retainer like Sir Goraev. Luc had told her not to run away but he had not licensed her to run into his arms the moment he returned. Which, Christina realised as her blood turned cold, was exactly what she had been about to do.

Her hand went to her mouth. 'You kiss me like a woman in love,' he had said. She had denied it. She had not believed it. But now she was faced with the evidence. She was in love with the clever, lying, utterly unattainable Prince of Kholkhastan.

'Hell,' she said. 'How could I be so *stupid*?'

She turned and ran in the opposite direction up the staircase to her own room. Here comes another sleepless night, she thought grimly.

Christina did not bother going to bed. She sat for a long time at the open window, looking out. The moon carved the landscape into little blocks of shadow. The stars looked cold. She could not stop shivering.

When had she fallen in love? That first day when she had realised she needed to keep something of her own private from him, even if it was only her designer traineeship? Or on the beach when they had so nearly made love? Or, worse than that, had she fallen in love with him in her own dreams?

Christina swore with rage and shame. Casting him as the hero of her fantasies was even more ridiculous than anything her mother had ever done. Silently she apologised to her mother's ghost. How she had winced when her mother had launched herself into another hopeless relationship, thinking that this time Prince Charming had arrived. Now she could understand it more easily.

'And I'm no better,' Christina told herself, pounding her fist on the window-sill until it hurt. 'I'm pathetic.'

Luc had given her no encouragement. At least, not to fall in love with him. He quite liked the idea of taking her to bed all right. But that was all. Why, almost the last thing he had said to her was not to bother learning to call his sister anything. That hardly sounded like a relationship with much of a future, Christina instructed herself grimly.

She was so absorbed in her thoughts that she did not hear the door open. Or turn her head to see the tall man silhouetted in the light from the hallway. For a moment he stood there watching her tense figure at the window. Then he spoke.

She nearly jumped out of the window with shock when Luc drawled, 'Waiting up for me, Christina?'

She sprang up from the window-seat and whirled to face him. He strolled in and closed the door deliberately behind him. Now the room had no light but the moon through the window, and it was leached of colour, loud with the sound of their breathing.

'What...?' Christina began in a breathless whisper.

Luc laughed. 'What am I doing here? Guess.'

Her heart began to thunder so loudly that she was certain he must hear it. She swallowed. She tried desperately to think of something to say to keep him at bay. Her mind was a complete blank.

He said softly, 'The last time I asked to spend the night with you, you told me you weren't that sort of girl.'

'I didn't. I said—not if you were the Emperor of China. Which you damn nearly are,' Christina retorted.

The night air hummed with warmth but she was shivering convulsively.

'So it's just as well that this time I'm not asking,' Luc said coolly.

He crossed the distance between them in two long strides. Expecting him to take her in his arms, Christina cried out in alarm as he swung her off her feet. He carried her to the undisturbed bed. In the moonlight, the thin, handsome face was laughing but very intent. She shut her eyes.

'This is pure melodrama,' she said with resolution. 'Put me down.'

'With pleasure,' he said courteously.

She was laid gently on the silky cover. Before she could move, however, or even had time to open her eyes, Luc was beside her.

'You've been fighting this from the first day we met,' he murmured. 'From the very first. It's nothing to be afraid of.'

Oh, but it is, thought Christina. When you feel the way I feel about a man who only wants what you want, there is everything in the world to be afraid of. Did I recognise that, subconsciously, the very first time you bought me coffee and told me selected truths that were worse than lies? How clever of me. So why wasn't I clever enough to get away?

Because she knew now that she was not going to get away. Her own body was ranged against her—to say nothing of her heart.

He kissed her until she was mindless. He did it with a slow, orchestrated artistry that was such a contrast to her own, almost unbearable excitement. Somewhere in the process he got rid of their clothes. But when she reached for him, writhing and nearly desperate, he held her at arm's length.

'Careful.' Luc was laughing but he was breathless too. 'We're supposed to be responsible adults, for God's sake. Time to think about safe sex.'

'What's safe about this?' Christina gasped. It came from the heart.

'Not very much, maybe, but all the more reason to take care of you...'

And he did. In every way there was. Clinging to Luc, Christina found herself climbing, soaring to heights she had never even imagined. It felt like the most dangerous thing she had ever done. And at the same time she had never felt so taken care of. She sobbed his name. Later, held warmly against him, she said it again, quietly, almost to herself, dazed with delight.

In the morning, of course, it was cold again and she was alone. Luc must have covered her up with the discarded bedclothes before he'd left, but her now naked skin shuddered in the cool morning breeze that came in from the open window. Christina hauled the covers up to her chin as she curled tightly into a ball and tried to pretend that she could get warm if she concentrated.

It was hopeless and she knew it. Luc had not even left her a note. He had gone, just as she had known he would. She would probably never feel warm again.

Eventually Christina got up and went downstairs, heavy-eyed. The kitchen was busy, but the Princess and her family were still asleep after the excitement of the day before, while the Prince had already gone out, one of the kitchen staff told her. The girl added that Sir Goraev was at work, however, and had asked if Christina would take in his morning tisane when she was ready.

This was said with a certain reservation but Christina did not notice in her new-found loneliness. She shrugged and took the tray that was offered.

He was sitting in Luc's study at the desk. He had a file open in front of him and he was frowning. As she crossed the room, Christina saw that the file contained press cuttings.

Sir Goraev looked up and gave her a polite smile. But his eyes looked worried, she saw.

'Your tisane,' she said.

'Thank you,' he said almost absently. He stood up and took it from her. 'Sit down, will you, Miss Howard?'

She did.

'What is it?' she asked quietly.

He bowed his head and picked up a paper-knife in the shape of a dagger. He studied it absorbedly. He did not raise his eyes when he spoke.

'My dear, I do not like to talk about your—private feelings,' he said at last.

Christina sat very still.

He seemed to wait for a response. When it did not come, he sighed faintly. 'If it were possible, I would not do so now. We hardly know each other. You will think it an impertinence. I do not like the necessity. But...'

He did look up then. And something in his face turned Christina's blood to ice.

'What is it?' she said in a croak. 'Luc—?'

An expression of pain flickered over his face and was gone. 'His Highness is perfectly well,' Sir Goraev said quickly. 'My poor child, do not look like that. I spoke to him only an hour ago at breakfast.'

He watched her sag in relief.

'I think perhaps I have been wrong,' he said slowly. 'I think perhaps you are in love with him.'

Christina winced and turned her head away, not answering. He sighed in quick impatience.

'Would it make it easier if I tell you that I know you spent the night with him?' he asked drily.

She flinched. Uncontrollable colour flooded her cheeks. A great wave of outrage washed over her. Was she allowed no privacy among these people?

'Is it part of your job to keep a log of the women he takes to bed, then?' Christina asked bitterly.

His lips compressed but he clearly decided not to take offence. 'I know it must feel an intrusion,' Sir Goraev said stiffly.

'It does,' she muttered.

His tone was a reproach. 'But—don't you see?—that only goes to show how unfit you are to be a companion to His Highness.'

'Companion! Why don't you call things by their real names, Sir Goraev,' she said with self-lacerating mockery. 'Don't you mean lover?'

He did not flinch. He looked at her gravely.

'I hope not.'

Her eyes were hard. 'Why not?'

'My dear—'

'And stop calling me that,' she said on a flash of temper. 'Why not?'

'You are young. You will get over this. I know you are very fond of His Highness now. But he is older than you. He lives in an entirely different world. You know this.' He drew a deep breath and said with regretful precision, 'One night with an attractive man does not make a love affair, you know. Especially when you come from such different worlds.'

Christina winced as if at a blow. She felt as if he had taken the little silver dagger he was still playing with and stabbed it into her heart. It made it all the worse that he was only echoing her own thoughts of this morning.

She shook her head slowly. She knew that she was mortally hurt but she could feel no wound yet. She drew a ragged breath and said harshly, 'I suppose Luc told you.'

He looked really shocked.

'My—' He stopped himself. 'Of course not. His Highness would not discuss such a matter with another.'

But she was so hurt that she did not believe him. She didn't say it. She didn't have to. Her continued suspicion offended him, she could see.

He said stiffly, 'Your personal dealings with His Highness are not within my remit. Such things are private, even for public men.'

Christina raised an eyebrow. 'Then what is this conversation about?'

He sighed impatiently. 'My dear Miss Howard, you are not a fool. His Highness keeps his feelings to himself.'

'Aren't we talking about his feelings?'

'No,' he said positively.

He gave her a steely look. Under the veneer of courtesy he had a job to do and he was determined to do it, Christina saw. It chilled what little warmth was left round her heart.

'Then—'

'We are talking about his duty, his commitments. And your feelings in so far as they pose a threat to those commitments,' he explained.

It was quite kindly said. It was very gentle. And utterly brutal.

'Commitments?' Christina said. It was not much more than a whisper.

'His Highness will, of course, need to marry.' Sir Goraev looked down at his little paper-knife. 'Hitherto it has not been a priority; he has had other responsibilities. Oh, he has had other relationships—discreetly—of course. Like that actress. But that is all over now.' An eloquent gesture of his well-kept hands consigned Juliette Legrain to insignificance. 'It did not concern his father. He knew that when the time came His Highness would do his duty.'

She did not doubt it either. Christina found that she was beginning to hate the word.

'After his father died, His Highness had much to do. It was a big change from orchestrating peace treaties for the UN. He has made the necessary adjustment. Now it is time to think of marriage.'

Christina felt numb. Shame flicked across her nerves like a whip. Her eyelids quivered. She looked down, unable to sustain the old man's regretful gaze.

'Who is he going to marry?' she muttered.

Sir Goraev moved sharply as if she had startled him. 'Do not trouble yourself with such things,' he said quickly. 'It does no good. You will only hurt yourself more.'

'But—'

'His Highness is an honourable man. He would not marry and ask you to accept a less secure role in his life,' he said, choosing his words with care. 'It would not be fair. You would not care for it. So there is no alternative. This little game between you has to come to an end.'

Christina said in a strangled voice, 'Did he tell you to tell me so?'

He shook his head, more in sorrow than indignation. 'How can you, who know him, ask me this? His Highness has not mentioned the matter to me. But—for your own sake, my child, as well as his—I advise you most earnestly to be gone when he returns. Partings are painful, even when one is not in love. And you, I think, are.'

Christina folded her lips together. She said nothing. There was nothing to say.

He sighed. 'This is all very different from when I was young,' he said.

He sounded angry. Christina saw suddenly that he was really upset by their conversation.

'In those days no decent woman made love with a man to whom she was not married. Or went off racketing round the world without someone to protect her, taking jobs here and there. It was all so much easier then. Why did everything have to change?'

He flung the knife down onto the desk as if it infuriated him.

'From your behaviour, one would say you were sophisticated. What is that word they use these days? Streetwise? Yes, that is it. Streetwise. That you know what you are doing and are willing to take the consequences. But it is all a pretence. You could not endure an irregular relationship with His Highness. And that is all he could offer you. It would break your heart.'

He did not say it would break Luc's heart, Christina noticed. She winced.

He went on in the same angry tone, 'If you were like that actress of his, he would give you a diamond or two and the two of you would have a pleasurable reunion every so often. It would be nothing to do with his marriage. Rather, a delightful little adventure for both of you, from time to time. Neither of you would be hurt for a moment. But you are not the type to handle a civilised affair like that. You think you are so independent and capable but in the dealings between a man and a woman you are a child.'

Christina moistened dry lips. 'If that were true,' she said quietly, 'we would not be having this conversation.'

The old man almost jumped. He looked at her, his eyes narrowed. 'Did you think he would *marry* you?' he said scornfully.

She got up swiftly, and made for the door. It disconcerted the old courtier. His voice sharpened to razor effect.

'Where are you going? I haven't finished.'

But his cutting tone had no effect on her. Christina could not bear it any longer. In spite of the old man's denial, she could see it all. When Luc had left her in bed this morning he must have gone down to breakfast and told his Lord Chamberlain all about it. Probably they had even discussed the possibility of her accepting—what had Goraev called it?—an irregular relationship. She could almost hear them, the two men of the world, discussing what was to be done about her unwanted, unsophisticated devotion to the Prince.

It was betrayal of the most profound kind. Nothing could hurt her worse than this. Christina found that she was shaking.

'I have,' she said.

She turned and faced him, taking hold of the doorknob between clammy fingers behind her back. The door was blessedly solid. She steadied herself against it. She was very white but her head was high.

'I did not realise I was making love with the entire royal household,' she said quietly. 'You're quite right, Sir Goraev. That's not my scene at all. I like rather more respect for personal feelings than the Prince's commitments seem to allow him.'

She could not say Luc's name. She wondered if she ever would again.

She added with gentle dignity, 'But I am glad I know where I stand. I suppose I should thank you.'

Sir Goraev did not look reassured.

'Miss Howard,' he began urgently.

'Goodbye,' she said.

CHAPTER TEN

CHRISTINA went back to Athens to Sue.

Her friend took one look at the blank expression in her eyes and put her to bed with a hot drink. Christina sat up against the pillows with her hands clutched round the mug. She could not stop shivering.

'You're ill,' said Sue.

But Christina shook her head. 'I'm in love.'

It was the first time she had said it out loud. It sounded like a death sentence. From Sue's expression she was thinking along the same lines.

'I promised I'd tell you when it happened,' Christina said with a bleak smile. 'Well, it has. And I don't want to talk about it.'

'But— Right,' said Sue, the best of friends. 'It's that guy at Costa's, right? Is he going to follow you again? Do you want me to fend him off?'

'You won't have to,' said Christina.

She leaned back among Sue's pretty, sprigged pillows, eyes closed. Silent tears poured down her cheeks. Sue looked at her in helpless sympathy. Christina opened her eyes.

'I'm all right,' she said. 'I just need this one cry and then I'll get on with things.'

Christina was as good as her word. After that first collapse she pulled herself together very creditably. Until her next job was due to start she found work as a waitress, and was determinedly cheerful every evening when Sue came back to the flat.

Every day Christina went to collect her post. Every day there was nothing from Luc and she felt the deso-

171

lation hit her again. I shall get over him, Christina vowed every morning on her way to the little café from the poste restante building. I *shall*.

By the end of the week she had lost five pounds, in spite of the café's excellent cooking, and collected double her wages in tips.

'Put it in the bank,' Sue had said, refusing to take any more than half the food bills. 'Friends don't pay rent. You'll need that money in the winter.'

So Friday morning saw her once more at the cashier's desk in the bank. The clerk blenched when he saw her and ducked down behind the counter. In spite of her general despondent conviction that her life was over, Christina could not help being amused.

'It's all right,' she told him. 'This time I'm paying money in. No more scenes.'

But in that she was wrong, even though she made no complaint about the inordinate time he seemed to take processing her simple transaction. As she reached the swing door, a hand fell on her shoulder. It was the security guard.

'Miss Howard?'

'Yes,' she agreed, bewildered.

'Will you come with me, please?'

She looked round at the interested eyes of the other customers and felt a quiver of alarm. What had she done? The security guard was not forthcoming. Instead he took her to a large, empty room with a large oval table in the middle of it and left her there. No explanation, no company, just walls full of photographs of directors and that great official table. Christina prowled round it, alarm giving way to anger.

When the door opened she swung round in a fury.

'What the *hell* is—?'

She was struck dumb. It was Luc.

'Thank you, Vassili,' he said to the bowing bank manager.

Christina closed her eyes. To think she had once thought that knowing a bank manager would solve all her troubles, she mused savagely. When she opened them, the bank manager had gone and Luc was standing in front of her. He was in his immaculate suit again and looking supremely handsome and unapproachable.

'Shall we go?'

'I won't go anywhere with you,' said Christina, refusing to be intimidated.

He sent her an unsmiling look.

'I'm afraid you'll have to,' he said coolly. 'I have no intention of making love to you on the boardroom floor. Or even this handsome table.'

Christina's jaw dropped. 'Make—? How dare you?' she said faintly.

He did smile then but it did not reach his eyes.

'When a man is desperate he will dare anything, Christina. You didn't leave me much alternative.'

Christina stared. Desperate?

'After all, you wouldn't have got in touch with me, would you? I left my private telephone number with that café owner, but you never picked it up.'

Clever, lying Luc *desperate*?

She cleared her throat. 'How do you know I didn't pick it up?' It came out as a croak.

'It was the first thing on my agent's agenda. Hotly followed by your address in Italy. Like I told you, he drew a blank on that too.'

She could not believe it.

He took a hasty step towards her. 'Do you know how many rules I broke for you, Christina? Have you any idea?'

She shook her head dumbly.

He shook his head too, his expression infinitely tired. 'No, you haven't, have you?' He paused, seeming to debate with himself. Then, making up his mind, he said deliberately, 'All my staff have been sending me memos about it for two months. The officials, the protocol people, the negotiators, the bodyguards.' He sent her a quick look. 'Did you realise we had company that first day we had coffee?'

She cast her mind back to the café.

'The man at the next table?' she asked slowly. 'The one who was pretending to read a newspaper? I knew he was looking at us. I thought it must be because you were famous. Was he secret service or something?'

'Something,' Luc said drily. 'And he wasn't supposed to be that obvious. You rather shocked him out of his professional cool, I'm afraid. Especially when you flung my money all over him.'

For the first time in days Christina grinned. It was a good memory. 'Did he go around the café picking it up?'

Luc was wry. 'He didn't know what to do. He was supposed to be undercover, so he ought not to have had any contact with me. On the other hand he was also supposed to make sure I wasn't robbed or insulted or otherwise done a violence to.' His eyes glinted. 'And you'd managed the hat trick. So you presented him with an unsolvable dilemma. It seems to be your speciality.'

'I didn't do you a violence,' Christina protested.

He looked at her consideringly. 'Didn't you?'

'A few bank notes—'

'I wasn't,' he said quietly, 'talking about the bank notes.'

And suddenly neither of them was laughing any more.

He said roughly, 'I shouldn't have taken you on as crew, you know that? You weren't cleared and none of the usual agencies could get a lead on you. I should never have had you tracked down and offered that job. They all thought I was mad.'

Christina was chilled. 'The officials and the bodyguards?'

'Particularly the officials. Goraev was so worried that he cancelled everything. That was why he joined us at the villa.'

Christina flinched, remembering that final interview with Sir Goraev all too vividly. 'I can imagine.'

'Yes.' Luc met her eyes. 'I didn't realise. I was a fool. You see, Goraev has a daughter and he was hoping we might make a match of it. I don't know the girl very well. It never crossed my mind.' He looked suddenly haunted. 'So it never occurred to me he would get rid of you like that. What can I say?'

Christina hid her hurt. She said in a light, hard voice, 'Think nothing of it. Though I don't see why he bothered. I imagine he's used to it.'

Luc's head came up. 'What do you mean by that?' he said grimly.

Christina thought of Sir Goraev's casual dismissal of the gorgeous Juliette. She took an angry step forward.

'Are you telling me he hasn't got rid of ladies for you before? When they were surplus to requirements, I mean.'

Luc whitened. There was a little silence.

'What did I ever do?' he said at last. He sounded stunned, as if he was in real pain—as if he could hardly believe it.

Christina swallowed. 'I got the impression he'd got rid of the actress,' she said, not entirely lucidly.

She could feel Luc's eyes boring into her. She refused to look at him. If she did he would see her whole heart in her eyes. She could not afford that. He was too clever. And her heart was too unguarded.

After a pause he said in a level voice, 'Then he misled you.'

That startled her. She looked up quickly. A muscle was working just below the prominent cheekbone. His expression was unreadable.

'I know, of course, the lady to whom you refer,' he said precisely. 'She is—a friend. For a while she was perhaps more than that. She is gorgeous and clever and—well, you have seen her.'

Gorgeous, amazingly poised, amazingly sexy. Everything that a student-cum-ship's cook was not. It hurt like an ice burn.

Christina could have sworn that she did not make a move, but his voice sharpened into urgency suddenly. 'I swear it was no more than that. For either of us.'

She shrugged, quite as if she did not care. Luc was not deceived.

'Believe me. I don't know what Goraev said—or what you thought you saw at that party—but it is all history.' He smote one hand down on another suddenly. 'Christina, please. You cannot reject me for nonsense like this. *Listen* to me.'

Reject him? What was he talking about?

But he misread her bewilderment. 'If you walk out on me now, I will follow,' he said fiercely. 'I'll never let you alone until you've given me a fair hearing.'

She was shaking. She pressed her hands together so that he wouldn't see.

'I'm listening.' It did not sound encouraging. It was not meant to.

Luc gave her a baffled look. 'Juliette and I—well, we were in the same boat. Both famous. Both followed by the paparazzi. She had her life and I had mine and we were both serious about our careers. They get lonely—careers. For a while—well, what can I say?—we salved each other's loneliness. It was not for ever and neither of us thought it was. She knows how I feel about you. I told her at that damned party. She wishes us both well. One day maybe she'll find the same thing.'

Christina looked away. She resisted the impulse to demand what exactly he hoped Juliette would find.

He said with abrupt anger, 'And, if Goraev told you he'd warned her off, he was lying. He has no right to speak for me in my private life. I never discussed Juliette with him or anyone else.' He paused. 'How can you think I would? I didn't even discuss her with you, for God's sake.'

'Even me?'

'If anyone had a right to know, you did.'

Christina said nothing.

After a moment he went on. 'My sister tells me she told you Juliette and I were lovers. Is that true?'

'She mentioned it, yes.'

'And you didn't ask me about it?'

'What chance did I get?' Christina said on a flash of temper. 'The only night we spent together, I don't remember us exchanging the stories of our lives.'

It might have been her imagination but she thought that the elegantly suited shoulders flinched.

Luc said quietly, 'You have a right to be angry.'

'Oh, I'm not angry,' Christina said lightly. 'Why should I be? I had the job of a lifetime. And a truly enriching personal experience to go with it.'

'Stop that,' he said, slapping his hand down flat on the polished table.

It sounded like a pistol shot. Christina jumped.

'You have every reason to be hurt. I accept it. I will deal with it. But I will not put up with cheap shots like that. I haven't deserved it and they aren't worthy of you.'

'Oh, aren't they?' said Christina, roused to combat at last. 'Not what you're used to, Your Highness? Am I supposed to bow politely and say thank you for turning my life upside down?'

His eyes gleamed. 'Did I?'

'Yes, you—' She recovered herself. 'You just might have done if I hadn't...' She met his eyes and looked quickly away. 'That is, if Sir Goraev hadn't explained the situation to me.'

'As I have just been saying, he did not understand the situation.' Luc sounded exasperated. 'So he certainly couldn't have explained anything.'

'Oh, I think he had a pretty fair idea,' Christina said with an irony that did nothing at all to conceal her hurt.

He took an impatient stride towards her. 'He is an old man. He just doesn't live in the present. His fantasy world is one part of the nineteen-twenties, three parts Strauss opera. He nearly ruined my sister's chances of putting her marriage back together with his nonsense. You can't let him do the same to us.'

Christina stared. All of a sudden her heart seemed to be beating so loudly that she could almost believe Luc could hear it. She said carefully, 'How could he have any effect on your sister's marriage?'

Luc looked irritated, but he answered patiently enough. 'My brother-in-law is a workaholic. When he is busy he forgets to spend time with her and the children. She complained. Sir Goraev told Richard to take no notice, she'd always been like that, she would forget it. As a result, Richard has been ignoring the problem and my poor sister has been playing with fire.'

Christina shook her head. 'I don't understand.'

'I think you understand very well,' Luc said shrewdly. 'From what Simon says, you saw her flirting with Stuart Define. You never mentioned it to me. Impressive discretion, that.'

Christina was not sure whether she was being laughed at. She said haughtily, 'I thought you were a grubby reporter.'

'A *grubby* reporter?' He sounded stunned.

'Extremely grubby,' she said with relish. 'I was trying to protect everyone from you.' She sent him a darkling look. 'By the time I realised the only one who needed protection was me, I didn't feel like telling you anything.'

Unexpectedly, his mouth quirked. 'I remember.'

'Anyway, I wouldn't have discussed the Princess's business.'

'Very right and proper.' Luc's tone was dry. 'The trouble is, if no one discussed it, how was my brother-in-law going to find out that his marriage was on the line? He wasn't there enough to see it for himself. And I was too full of my own affairs to notice.'

He looked at her broodingly. The hammer blows of her heart became deafening.

Christina said with constraint, 'I take it they have sorted out their differences now?'

'They're beginning to. Mainly thanks to Simon's bolt for freedom. They've talked it through and realised that neither of them wants the sort of polite, semi-detached marriage that Goraev thinks people like us ought to have.'

'Oh,' said Christina.

The all-perceptive retainer was beginning to shrink to human size. Inexplicably, her spirits rose comparably.

'You make him sound like a complete busybody.'

'That's right,' said Luc.

'But— I thought you took his advice. I thought he knew *everything*.'

'So did he.'

He sounded so impatient that Christina's heart lifted a couple of notches further.

'But you did tell him to get reports on me?'

He spread his hands. 'Security checks, I said. They're not just specific to you. Everyone that works for us has had them.'

She nodded. 'I see.'

Luc's eyes flickered. 'When we went to the villa, it was the first time I'd had the chance to talk to Goraev for a month. I told him I already knew everything about you I needed to know,' he said quietly. 'And I didn't get it from a secret-service report.'

Christina began to feel breathless all of a sudden. Her eyes fell.

'But Sir Goraev didn't agree?'

Luc showed his teeth. 'Apparently not. We—er—discussed it. After you'd gone. It was rather an unpleasant interview. In the end Goraev agreed that the reports showed enough to satisfy him that you weren't going to blow us all up or kidnap the children.'

He paused, not taking his eyes off her.

'But, you see, the trouble was that that hadn't been what he'd been afraid of once he had seen you.' He reached out and touched her face, making her look at him. He held her eyes. His own were unfathomably dark. 'And seen me.'

Quite suddenly Christina began to tremble. All her laminated nonchalance melted as if touched by a flame.

'I don't know what you mean,' she said, almost voiceless.

'He knew that I was in love with you,' Luc said evenly. 'He knew I wanted to marry you.'

Christina found that she could think of nothing at all to say. She did not believe him. Of course she did not. And yet—though his eyes were masked and his mouth was under rigid control, that little muscle in his cheek was flickering again. And he was not laughing; she knew that for certain.

She stood as if turned to stone. Luc did not touch her.

But he said in a voice that he seemed to keep level only with an amazing effort, '*Now* can we please go?'

She went past him out of the door without a word. Luc put a hand on her elbow. Christina stiffened but he was only guiding her towards a lift.

It echoed through her mind: 'He knew I wanted to marry you.' Wanted? Did that mean he did not want to any more? Her mouth twisted in fierce self-mockery. Not now that she had proved conclusively that she was that sort of girl by spending a night of ecstasy in his arms.

She looked at Luc sideways. He looked appallingly grim—nothing at all like a man on the brink of a proposal of marriage. She could not deceive herself. He looked as if he almost hated her.

He took her to a courtyard she had not seen before.
As soon as they went out into the harsh sunlight, a man
in a chauffeur's uniform got out of a dark limousine.
It was Michael. This time Christina recognised the car
too. It temporarily displaced her tormented confusion.

'It *was* you chasing me that night.'

Luc moved his shoulders as if trying to cast off an
unpalatable memory.

'I apologise for that,' he said in a clipped voice. Clearly
he did not relish apologising. 'At the time I could not
think of another way to keep track of you.'

'Oh.'

How could he have wanted to marry her? He hardly
knew her. They were worlds apart. Her thoughts whirled.

This time he did not pretend that the car was not his,
or dispense with the chauffeur.

'The hotel, Michael.'

The chauffeur held one of the heavy doors open for
her. She slipped in, flushing slightly. Luc got in beside
her and Michael closed the door on him with a faint
thud. Christina swallowed and said the first thing that
came into her head.

'Your car has the heaviest doors I've ever come across.'

Luc gave an odd little grimace. 'Bulletproof, I'm
afraid.'

'*Oh!*'

She was shocked. It had never occurred to her. Nothing
could have underlined more completely the difference
between them, Christina thought numbly. She said
nothing on the rest of the journey to Athens's premier
hotel.

She was still in a state of shock when he took her up
to the luxury suite and dismissed the hovering secretary.
As soon as the man had gone Luc swung round on her
as if he could contain himself no longer.

'The first time I saw you,' he said. 'The very first
time. Do you remember?'

'I hit you with a revolving door,' Christina said literally. She was completely at sea and feeling faintly intoxicated by it.

'You hit me with more than that.' He punched his fist into his open palm. 'I've never behaved like this before, believe me. Never felt like this. I know you think I'm high-handed but I have never felt I had to move so fast before. I couldn't afford to let you get away. Do you understand?'

Christina did not dare to. 'No.'

Luc said quietly, 'Do you remember saying that we could afford to be honest with each other because we wouldn't meet again?'

For some reason tears were pricking at the corner of her eyes. Christina nodded, wordless.

'Well, that's how I thought it was. A pretty girl who didn't know who I was. A morning at a café table, forgetting my responsibilities. Just being a normal man talking to a normal girl about the tourist sights and the wonderful light. Flirting a little. The sort of casual, fun conversation I haven't had for twenty years. Even less so since I inherited. I was doing what other men do and enjoying it. Only...' He hesitated.

Christina held her breath.

'It wasn't like that,' he said at last, abruptly.

She moistened suddenly dry lips.

'What made it different?' Her voice was a croak.

'I don't know. It may have been when you said crewing was your bid for freedom. It was a long time since I'd felt free. Or even thought about it. It struck a chord, that. I'd never met anyone like you.'

He fell silent, his dark face brooding. Christina wanted to touch it. She did not quite dare. She locked her hands together hard. She struggled to make her voice normal.

'Not used to women who don't fall at your feet?' she mocked.

But he did not laugh in return. 'Not used to women who treat their prejudices like a religion,' he said harshly. 'When we met on the quayside you couldn't wait to tell me what a disaster the Prince of Kholkhastan was. You did not even know that you had met me and yet you decided I was a villain, sight unseen. And nothing was going to change your mind.'

Her chin came up. 'So you set out to change my mind, did you?' Christina challenged him coolly. 'What did you think would do it? Your lying to me? Or your seducing me?'

Luc stared at her, baffled and furious. 'I told you. I wanted you to see me as I was, damn it.' He shouted suddenly, 'Was that too much to ask?'

Christina thought, I've never heard him raise his voice before, not even when he sacked Demetrius. He just gets cold and deadly. And now he's shouting like an ordinary man. It came to her slowly: an ordinary man at the end of his tether.

'Desperate?' she said, suddenly believing it.

Luc gave a harsh, unamused laugh. 'Completely.'

'Then when you seduced me—'

'We made love, for God's sake,' he interrupted furiously. 'You and me mutually. I thought— That's one area where we meet as equals. Never mind the advance publicity, never mind the prejudices. In bed it's just you and me not pretending.'

Christina was awed to silence.

Luc took a hasty step towards her. He still did not touch her but when he looked into her eyes his expression was naked.

'Was I wrong, Christina?' he said quietly. 'Were you pretending, after all?'

She scanned the thin, handsome face. That haughty brow could be so intimidating. Luc didn't look intimidating now. He looked as if he was being tortured. Wonderingly Christina put out a hand.

It was seized and held fiercely until the bones nearly cracked.

She said softly, 'Desperate for *me*?'

Luc closed his eyes. 'I'm not sure I can live without you,' he said simply. He opened his eyes. 'I was always afraid you'd run once you realized how I felt. That's why I told you to wait for me when I went to look for Simon. I wasn't sure you would. When I came back and you were still there—well, I went a little mad, I think. Most uncharacteristic.' He gave a bitter laugh. 'I'm famed for my self-control. But with you...' He shrugged. 'Well, you've seen.'

Christina said shakily, 'I can't pretend to be what I'm not.'

He looked as if she had stabbed him.

'I mean I'm not in your class. All those clever, international types at your party, to say nothing of the film stars— I'm not like that.' She struggled to put what she meant into words. 'It's just like when we were swimming. You should have beaten me but you chose not to. I can't live like that. Everyone would be making allowances for me all the time. I—'

Luc put out his hand and touched the back of it to her hot cheek. Christina fell abruptly silent, her eyes brimming with panicky tears.

'Darling, listen to me. I told you being a prince was a performance. Well, the performance has been taking me over. All those film stars, no doubt.' His smile was bitter.

Christina rubbed a fist over her face and sniffed. 'I don't understand.'

'You should. It was you who made me realise—most of all when you burst in that day and made me see what Goraev was doing to my humanity. You were right. Simon was more important than all the protocol in the world.' His face twisted suddenly. 'Do you know, when I found him, he said he hadn't talked to me about his parents because he thought I'd be too busy doing important things?'

Christina nodded. 'He told me princes have to do things they don't want to. And that you didn't have any fun any more.'

'He saw what was happening to me more clearly than I did. I owe young Simon.' He paused. 'And you. You thought I hid who I was because I wanted a brief affair. You were so wrong. What I was had become a sort of prison. I was beginning to see that. You'd escaped from your prison. I didn't want to pull you back into mine.'

He took her hand.

Christina said in a choked voice, 'You said you wouldn't pretty things up. If you want to go to bed with me, why don't you just say so?'

Her hand was crushed. He hauled her towards him.

'Christina,' he said quietly.

She moistened her lips. 'Yes.'

'Look at me.'

'I—'

'Look at me.'

She did. His eyes were gleaming with a light that she had never seen before. She could not look away.

He drew a long breath and said carefully, 'Do you love me?'

There was no point in pretending.

'Yes,' she said simply.

He let out a long breath of sheer relief. 'Then you'll marry me.'

'But—'

'Or I shall pursue you till you do.'

'You can't. You don't know where I live.'

'I've got your box number in Milan,' he said. His eyes were dancing suddenly. 'I shall camp there till you pick up your mail.'

She stared, taken aback.

'It's going to cost me a whole series of interviews with that appallingly keen young student friend of yours.'

Christina was even more bewildered. 'Karl? What—? Why—?' She gave up, flinging up her hands in defeat.

Luc laughed. 'He was very suspicious at first. Swore that he didn't know how to get hold of you out of the season. Only when I made it clear how I felt—and that it was for ever—did he agree to find out. The trouble was, he had a price.' He sighed dramatically. 'I never give personal interviews, on principle. If my colleagues at the UN heard about it, they wouldn't believe it. Don't you forget, my girl, I've done more for you than I would do for anyone or anything else in the world. But it will be worth it. You're never going to get away from me again.'

'I can't marry you,' Christina said, shaken.

'If you love me, I defy you to do anything else.'

She saw with wonder that in spite of his amused tone Luc was deadly serious. As if he could not help himself, he put up his hand and smoothed the soft tangle of brown hair back from her face.

'You mean it,' she whispered.

He pulled her into his arms. 'Oh, my darling.'

'But you don't approve of me. I speak my mind and I crew and I lose my temper with bank clerks,' she said in a muffled voice.

He was kissing the vulnerable skin below her ear.

'Very entertaining,' he said, laughter quivering in his voice.

She shivered with pleasure. 'I'm another appallingly keen student,' she warned. 'Of design. I'm based in Milan but I've got a visiting studentship with a Paris house.'

'We'll fit it into the itinerary,' Luc promised. He had reached her mouth. Christina stopped even trying to think. She gave herself up to his kiss.

'I thought you didn't want me,' she said on a gasp when he raised his head.

He looked blank. 'Didn't *want* you?' His shoulders began to shake. 'What do I have to do, for heaven's sake?'

Suddenly Christina felt all her doubts slip away. It was going to be all right. He loved her. Luc really loved her. She smiled at him brilliantly. 'Make love to me.'

He stared, fascinated. 'It will take some exceptional sapphires to match those eyes. We must do something about that.'

Christina pretended to frown. 'Make *love* to me.'

He suppressed a smile. 'Only if you agree to marry me as soon as I can arrange it.'

'You drive a hard bargain.'

He looked modest. 'International negotiating skills. Years of training.'

'Oh.' She pondered. 'In that case—I suppose it would be quicker to agree now and get it over with.'

Luc's hold tightened but he chuckled. 'I could persuade you,' he murmured in her ear.

Christina gave a long sigh of pure pleasure and gave herself up into his embrace. She met eyes so full of warmth that they dazzled her.

'I'm persuaded,' she said. 'Marriage it is. As long as you make love to me as well.'

Luc laughed aloud. 'It's a deal,' he said.

He swung her off her feet and carried her through the suite to a room full of gold leaf and chandeliers. Christina did not notice anything but the canopied bed. Then Luc dropped her onto it and she lost awareness of everything but him.

She reached up to him. The laughter died out of his eyes. Christina knew that she must have that same look of unguarded feeling. In this, as he had said, they were equals. Her hands closed round his shoulders and brought him down to her.

'Burn, fire, burn,' she said.

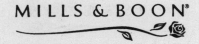

MILLS & BOON®

Next Month's Romances

♡

Each month you can choose from a wide variety of romance with Mills & Boon. Below are the new titles to look out for next month in our two new series Presents and Enchanted.

Presents™

ONE-MAN WOMAN	Carole Mortimer
MEANT TO MARRY	Robyn Donald
AUNT LUCY'S LOVER	Miranda Lee
HIS SLEEPING PARTNER	Elizabeth Oldfield
DOMINIC'S CHILD	Catherine Spencer
JILTED BRIDE	Elizabeth Power
LIVING WITH THE ENEMY	Laura Martin
THE TROPHY WIFE	Rosalie Ash

Enchanted™

NO MORE SECRETS	Catherine George
DADDY'S LITTLE HELPER	Debbie Macomber
ONCE BURNED	Margaret Way
REBEL IN DISGUISE	Lucy Gordon
FIRST-TIME FATHER	Emma Richmond
HONEYMOON ASSIGNMENT	Sally Carr
WHERE THERE'S A WILL	Day Leclaire
DESERT WEDDING	Alexandra Scott

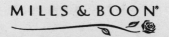

MILLS & BOON®

We value your comments!

Please spare a few moments to fill in the following questionnaire.
NO STAMP NEEDED.

Last month we introduced two new cover designs for our romance
novels—Presents and Enchanted—and we'd like to know what you
think. Please tick the appropriate box ☑ to indicate your answers.

---

1. How long have you been a Mills & Boon Romance reader?

Less than 1 year ☐   1-2 years ☐   3-5 years ☐
6-10 years ☐   Over 10 years ☐

2. How many Mills & Boon Romances do you read/buy in a month?

	Read	Buy
1-4	☐	☐
5-8	☐	☐
9-12	☐	☐
13-16	☐	☐
Over 17	☐	☑

3. From where do you usually obtain your Mills & Boon Romances?

Mills & Boon Reader Service ☐
WH Smith/John Menzies/Other Newsagent ☑
Supermarket ✓ ✓ ☐
Borrowed from a friend ☐
Bought from a second-hand shop ☐
Other (please specify) _____

*4. Thinking about the **Presents** cover do you:*

Like it very much ☐   Don't like it very much ☐
Like it quite a lot ☐   Don't like it at all ☐

Please turn over ☞

5. *Thinking about the* **Enchanted** *cover do you:*

Like it very much ☐   Don't like it very much   ☐

Like it quite a lot ☐   Don't like it at all   ☐

6. *Do you have any additional comments you'd like to make about the Presents and Enchanted covers?*

_____

_____

7. *It is intended that the two new covers will help readers to distinguish between the different types of romantic storylines, do you think this is a good idea?*

Yes ☐   No ☐

8. *Are you a Reader Service subscriber?*

Yes ☐   No ☐

9. *Please indicate your age group*

16-24 ☐   25-34 ☐   45-54 ☐   55-64 ☐   65+ ☐

Thank you for your help

Please send your completed questionnaire to:

Harlequin Mills & Boon Ltd.,
Presents/Enchanted Questionnaire,
Dept. M, FREEPOST, P.O. Box 183,
Richmond, Surrey, TW9 1ST

E1

Ms/Mrs/Miss/Mr _____

Address _____

_____

_____ Postcode _____